D0423417

Endorsements

"Come to the Garden is a creative, well-written, and inspiring spiritual autobiography penned by Ms. Jennifer Morgan. Correlating her rich and varied experience of personal dreams with biblical passages and stories, Ms. Morgan offers the reader an in-depth look into a rare and fascinating faith journey. Believers and seekers alike will be drawn into this narrative of a growing relationship with God through life's challenges and celebrations. Ms. Morgan's invitation to her backyard garden is well-worth accepting!"

—The Rev. Dr. Theodore M. Smith,
coordinator of Congregational Care &
theological consultant
Krist Samaritan Center
Houston, Texas

"This is a garden you will enter and never want to leave. Come sit, be uplifted, and learn with Jennifer the rewards of slowing down and enjoying the presence of God!"

—Sharon Hargrove, wife of former Major
League Baseball player and manager Mike
Hargrove and author of the book, *Safe at
Home: A Baseball Wife's Story.*
Cleveland, Ohio

"Some years ago, as a novice spiritual director, I quickly realized that I was sitting in the presence of a modern mystic, a woman specially gifted with living in a thin place, where the veil between the here and the not-here trembles with anticipation of new encounters with the Divine. Jennifer Morgan has courageously lived into the numinous experiences offered to her over the years. You can believe absolutely in the holy dreams and visions that she has skillfully woven into this luminous novel. Her words and images fairly dance across the pages, inviting others into deepening awareness. Welcome to the garden—Jennifer's garden—where you will find self-revealing honesty and extraordinary faith."

—Constance Bovier, author of *More God*, *From the Crucible*, and *Restoring Hope*
Houston, Texas

"My initial motivation to read an early draft of Jennifer Morgan's first novel was curiosity as an aspiring writer myself. But I soon felt a burning need to put aside everything else I was reading and devour this amazing book that pours a uniquely gifted woman's lifelong spiritual journey into an inspired, autobiographical-fictional style. It's as down home and entertaining as Jan Karon, yet as penetrating as Frank Perretti. Will guys like this book as much as gals will? If they've ever wondered if God still reveals Himself to us today and what it might be like to talk to one of His angels who loves good coffee—Yes!"

—Tom Stoerzbach, marketing writer/editor
Houston, Texas

"Come to the Garden is an intriguing story told through the eyes of author, Jennifer Morgan, and her guardian angel, Margaret. I was hooked from the first page. As Jennifer shares with the wise, funny, coffee-loving angel her experiences with listening to God's voice, you cannot help but be drawn into the intimacy of the setting.

It's a beautiful book that made me laugh out loud, it made me cry, and I did not want to put it down. The book inspires us to take the time to listen for God's voice, because we are all children of God and He is speaking to us."

—Louise Kramer, director of Music Ministries,
The Woodlands United Methodist Church
The Woodlands, Texas

"Regarding Come to the Garden: The book gives a clear and interesting way of bringing out the author's testimony of God's faithfulness in never leaving or forsaking her through some very difficult trials."

—André Thornton,
former Major League Baseball player,
author of *Triumph Born of Tragedy*, and
president & CEO of ASW Global,
Akron, Ohio

Jennifer Wilder Morgan

A Novel Inspired by True Events

Come to the

Garden

TATE PUBLISHING
AND ENTERPRISES, LLC

Published by Tate Publishing & Enterprises, LLC
127 E. Trade Center Terrace | Mustang, Oklahoma 73064 USA
1.888.361.9473 | www.tatepublishing.com

Tate Publishing is committed to excellence in the publishing industry. The company reflects the philosophy established by the founders, based on Psalm 68:11,

"The Lord gave the word and great was the company of those who published it."

Book design copyright © 2013 by Tate Publishing, LLC. All rights reserved.
Cover design by Rtor Maghuyop
Interior design by Jomar Ouano

Published in the United States of America

ISBN: 978-1-62563-302-6
1. Fiction / Christian / General
2. Fiction / Biographical
12.12.17

Dedication

To my Abba Father God, who is the delight of my heart.

Acknowledgments

My heartfelt thanks go out to Constance Bovier, author and *Charis* Spiritual Director; Theodore Smith, D. Min.; and editor friend Kay Walter who provided invaluable spiritual guidance and review of my manuscript from its earliest days.

My "angels" of encouragement were many and include Lisa and Charles Chopp, Gaye Craig, Julie Huchton, Louise Kramer, Carey Little, Debbie McLin, Betty McNairy, Jill Moody, Margie Oden, Jenni Reilly, Tom and Diana Stoerzbach, Marsha West, my parents Sara and Bill Wilder, sister Carolyn Rose and brother Stewart Wilder, sister-in-law Mary Kirkpatrick and my aunt Adrienne and uncle Don Badgley. Your prayers and enthusiasm for this project, sound advice, and personal reviews of many versions of this book have blessed me and helped me more than you know.

I also want to express my sincere gratitude to Wes Hackney and Native Texas Landscape for sharing my love of creating spectacular spaces from the raw materials God provides. My beautiful gardens and the wildlife they attract were the inspiration for the setting of the events in this book.

And finally, to my husband, Guy, I thank you with a full and joyous heart. You have stood with me throughout this entire project and have been my faithful cheerleader. Your insights and advice have been invaluable to me, and I have loved sharing this experience with you. You are, and always have been, my hero.

Contents

Introduction

This book is written in a style that combines truth and fiction. My guardian angel, Margaret, is fictional; and her use in this story was suggested to me in a dream. I named her after a longtime friend and faithful Christian woman named Margaret Edwards, who recently celebrated ninety-six years of life. The events that take place in my backyard gardens with Margaret and her two angel friends are fictional. The life experiences and dream visions I share with her are true. All illustrations are my own original watercolor paintings.

Margaret

Are not all angels spirits in the divine service, sent to serve for the sake of those who are to inherit salvation?

Hebrews 1:14 (NRSV)

A wispy breath of air played across my face, just enough to tickle my nose and creep across my cheeks. I heard a faraway whisper. It was so faint that I strained to hear, but I just…couldn't…quite…catch up with it.

I awakened with a start. *Did someone just call my name?* Lifting my head, I looked around the room. The Texas sun was streaming through the plantation shutters on my bedroom windows, and the house was quiet. Sleepily I decided it must be my imagination and flopped back down into my pillow. But I couldn't go back to sleep. Something felt different. *I am not alone.*

A tiny knot of concern crept its way into my stomach, and as my other senses fully awakened, I became aware of a strange scent. Eyes closed, I inhaled deeply, trying to place the vague hint of something in the air. *Roses!* It smelled like my favorite white roses!

Where in the world is that coming from? I heard the soft jingle of a dog collar, and this time, I propped myself up on my elbows and looked over to where my Whippet, Cody, was nestled in his bed on the floor. His head was up, nose tilted to the ceiling, inquisitively sniffing the air. *Hm…I am not imagining things. He smells it, too*!

Curiosity won over the desire to pull the covers over my head and ignore this, so I climbed out of bed and slipped into a robe, careful not to disturb my other two dogs still snuggled in their beds. Cody leapt to his feet, ears perked at attention, and together we padded quietly through the house. The smell of roses was much stronger as we entered the kitchen. Nose still in the air, Cody trotted over and sat by the backdoor while I continued through the house in search of the source of this mysterious scent. My senses were on full alert as I peeked into closets, peered around doorways and into rooms but found nothing.

Perplexed, I headed back toward the kitchen where the scent was most intense. As I entered the kitchen, a brilliant flash of light caught my eye, and my attention was drawn to the windows looking out into the backyard. A shimmer of blue sparkled once, twice, three times between the columns in the garden beside the pool and fire pit. Edging closer to the window to get a better look, I heard an odd sound. It sounded like laughter—soft, musical laughter! It was coming from everywhere at once, but I still could not see anything. A slight chill ran up my spine, and my skin tingled as if the air was charged with electricity. Suddenly, Cody began to whine and paw frantically at the door.

"What is it, boy? Is something out there?"

Cody answered back with a sharp *ruff!* Hesitantly I opened the door for him and could barely push it all the way open before he bolted outside and disappeared from sight.

At that very moment, a sudden rush of wind blew in through the door. Knocked off balance, I stumbled backward into the kitchen as the door slammed itself shut. The wind softened in its intensity and moved to encircle me. Now I *knew* I was not alone! As I stood embraced in this oddly peaceful, warm whirlwind, I was aware that it carried with it the strong scent of white roses. There was an extraordinary gentleness about this wind as it caressed my face, lifted and tossed my hair, and playfully twisted and ruffled my robe and nightgown. And there was something else in the wind—*a presence*. There was a deep sense of invitation in this gentle tempest, as if it were calling my name and ever so delicately encouraging me to step outside. With trembling hands, I opened the door again and slowly walked out onto the back porch, propelled by this strange wind. My heart pounded in anticipation... of what?

As I stepped outside, I heard a soft giggle. Turning my head to follow the sound, my gaze fell upon the table and chairs arranged next to the garden. Cody stood there, panting happily as if to say "Look what I found, Mom!" My heart momentarily stopped as I witnessed the source of his excitement. There, standing by the table under the large blue patterned umbrella, was the loveliest woman I have ever seen!

Her radiant face was framed in a halo of soft, wavy pure white hair, and her blue eyes twinkled merrily. She was dressed in a cornflower blue gown that sparkled as if encrusted with thousands of tiny diamonds.

"Good morning, Jennifer!" She giggled softly again. Her smile radiated pure joy. "I'll bet you are surprised to see me!"

Surprised didn't even begin to describe what I was feeling. My mouth dropped open, and I stood frozen in midstep. I realized the wind that had carried me outside had disappeared.

"My name is Margaret, dear one, and I am your guardian angel! I have had the blessed privilege of watching over you your entire life."

Somehow, deep down, I knew she was speaking the truth. My mind spun as I tried to comprehend what was happening.

"Y...Y...You're an *angel*? Like, the *heaven* kind of... of angel?" I stammered in disbelief.

"That would be me!" This angel named Margaret nodded, her eyes sparkling merrily. I could tell she was enjoying this moment immensely.

"What a special day this is!" she continued. "Happy fiftieth birthday to you, Jennifer!" With a jolt, I came back to my senses. *My birthday!* I had completely forgotten!

Margaret laughed gently at my startled expression and said, "Come on over here, dear girl, you need to sit down. You are looking a bit shell-shocked! Come sit with me in your beautiful garden." She gathered her gown about her with one hand and sat down in one of the chairs, patting the chair next to her with her other hand.

Cody playfully scampered away as I walked over to the table and gratefully slid into the empty chair. Margaret was right—my knees did feel a little weak.

"I had completely forgotten about my birthday," I admitted shyly. "I guess I was a little distracted this morning by the house smelling of roses! Thank you for remembering."

"How could I not remember?" Margaret said. "I was here with you the night you celebrated with a beautiful garden party. It was such a nice evening, Jennifer. I love how you have celebrated this milestone in your life. Many choose to ignore it, at the very least!"

As Margaret spoke, I let my gaze wander over the backyard, and my thoughts returned to the recent evening when family and friends gathered to celebrate with me and my husband as we hosted my dream garden party. Tables set on the lawn were adorned with white linen tablecloths, votive candles, and lovely flower arrangements. And the food! We dined on a scrumptious barbecue feast including the best bacon-wrapped shrimp this side of the Mississippi. Oh, what a wonderful time of fellowship we all had!

"You're right, Margaret," I replied, breaking my reverie. "I truly have celebrated turning fifty. This is a happy and contented time in my life, and I am blessed with wonderful family and friends. God has been so good to me!"

"Yes, he has, child, and he loves you so very much." Margaret reached over and took one of my hands in hers. "And that is why I am here this morning. My presence is a special birthday gift to you from your Heavenly

Father. I understand that, for some time, your heart has wanted to tell a very special story, yet you have been, shall we say, somewhat hesitant? Worried about how you will accomplish this task? Our Father has heard your worries, dear one, and he sent me here to help you!" She smiled and gave my hand an encouraging squeeze.

"Wow, I can't believe you know about that," I admitted with a slightly embarrassed grimace. "For several years, there has been a growing desire in my heart to take on what is for me a rather surprising project. This desire, which began as a whisper, has grown increasingly insistent. The project, this great big leap out of my comfort zone, is to write a book. Margaret, I don't know the first thing about how to write a book!"

As soon as these words left my mouth, a stunning realization hit me. Not long ago, after months of fretting and worrying about how I was supposed to carry out this bewildering desire, I had a dream. In my dream, I heard the voice of my Lord say very succinctly, "Use an angel!" Upon awakening, I thought, *What a cool idea, but how am I going to do that?* Pushing the thought aside, I attributed it to being just a silly dream.

Gulp! Now, sitting here under the umbrella with my beautiful visitor, I realized it was not such a silly dream after all.

Tears of relief and gratitude welled in my eyes as I beheld this lovely gift from heaven sitting beside me.

"Oh, Margaret"—I breathed in wonder—"it's you! You are the angel! The one God told me about in my dream!"

The Assignment

All Scripture is inspired by God and is useful for teaching, for reproof, for correction, and for training in righteousness, so that everyone who belongs to God may be proficient, equipped for every good work.

2 Timothy 3:16–17 (NRSV)

Margaret laughed delightedly, and I was struck by how unusual and otherworldly her voice sounded, as if accompanied by the sound of tiny chimes.

"Yes, dearest child, I am the angel God has sent to you, and I am thrilled to be sitting with you here face-to-face after all these years. You have no idea what this means to me!"

I could only smile and shake my head. God is truly amazing.

"So tell me what you want to write about in this book of yours," said Margaret.

I gave her a quizzical look. "Don't you already know?"

"Humor me!" she said with a grin.

"My heart, Margaret, has been moved to provide a very personal answer to the question I have heard posed by so many people throughout my life: 'Where is God and why doesn't he speak to us anymore?'

"My answer to that question is that God is very much alive and present in our world today. He loves us, he *is* speaking to us, and most importantly, *he wants to be heard.*"

I looked over at Margaret, who was nodding her head in agreement. Her eyes sparked with an intensity that was not there a moment before, and I heard something resembling a low rumble of thunder echo in the distance as she began to speak. "Your desire, Jennifer, to tell others about how God speaks to you *comes from the desire of the Spirit that lives within you to be heard!* There is a scripture in the Book of Amos that counsels, "'Behold, the days are coming,'" declares the Lord God, "when I will send a famine on the land—not a famine of bread, nor a thirst for water, but of hearing the words of the Lord'" (Amos 8:11 ESV). Sadly, this is true for a great many people in the world you live in."

Encouraged by the profound truth in her words, I continued. "For me, discovering God and hearing his voice was not a thunderous-voice-booming-from-the-clouds event. Instead, God made himself known gently and gradually as I grew up. Then, as I actively began to seek a full-blown relationship with him, his presence and counsel gained in depth and intensity. And at times, his revelations have been so intense that they have rocked my world. His voice is now a treasured and trusted part of my everyday life. He guides, advises, and protects, sometimes with life-saving counsel.

"During these past fifty years, I have excelled and failed miserably. I have stumbled and picked myself up. I have negotiated paths that were clear and straight and paths that had unforeseen forks in the road. And as I lived through these experiences, I discovered that God had provided me with spiritual gifts or tools that would help me to live the life that he had ordained for me. When I gave my life to him, he took complete ownership. He taught me how to use my spiritual gifts and began to work his will through me. All that was required of me was to listen, to obey, and to trust. It took me a long time to learn how to do that!"

I continued with a thought that had been troubling me. "The reason I have been hesitant to move forward with this project pertains to something that is wonderful and amazing *and* unconventional. One of the most powerful ways that God speaks to me is through dream visions, which began in my teenage years. For reasons of his own, God decided to communicate with me primarily while I sleep."

I shot a rueful glance at Margaret. "Probably." I sighed. "Because my waking mind is far too cluttered with everyday trivialities!" An adorable snicker-snort erupted from Margaret, accompanied by a slight rolling of the eyes—she obviously knows me pretty well!

"Anyway, I have been reluctant until now to write about these visions because I know I will be stepping way outside of boundaries that many people call 'normal.' As a matter of fact, I know there will be those that will not take me seriously. But, Margaret, *I know* these dream visions are real. They are not made up, fairy-tale stuff. Visions are one of the spiritual gifts that God has given to me. I have experienced them for many years, they are very powerful, and I know without question that God is speaking to me. I have come to the realization that God has reasons for the gifts he gives to each of his children. He knows us intimately, he knows our hearts, and he gifts accordingly. I have also learned that it may take a lifetime to understand them. And the most wonderful thing of all, Margaret, is that when we begin to use our spiritual gifts in this world, we see that God is truly among us!"

Margaret's intense blue eyes looked deeply into mine. "Your own assurance, Jennifer, that your gifts are real is all you need to proceed with this very special project. Trust that whisper in your heart and trust in God to lead you. When you open your heart and become vulnerable to him, he will lead you to places you never dreamed of going!

"I am humbled that our Father has sent me to help you bring an important message to those who need to hear it. God *does* speak to people all over the world every day, in many different ways. Many realize it and have wonderful testimonies to tell, but a great many more do not. His voice is discounted as 'conscience,' 'coincidence,' 'intuition,' or 'imagination.' It is imperative, dear child, that all the people of the earth learn to listen to God's voice, because he is the source of life and truth. Heaven grieves for the despair of those who are living without God's loving presence in their lives. Those who do not know God have much to lose and everything to gain! We wholeheartedly rejoice in the knowledge that it is still not too late for any of his precious children to know him, to hear his voice and to experience the blessings and wonders of his kingdom."

Margaret reached over and gave my hand another encouraging squeeze. "So it seems that we both have our assignments. My directions are to help you stay focused, organized and *to keep your story based in Holy Scripture,* because the truths God has been revealing to you throughout your life come straight from his Holy Word. And I know of a particular scripture that will start this project off splendidly. Listen! 'The secret things belong to the Lord our God, but the things that are revealed belong to us and to our children forever, that we may do all the words of this law' (Deuteronomy 29:29 ESV). How wonderful that you are about to share with God's children the important truths he has revealed to you! I say we approach this assignment with joy and great anticipation! Are you in?"

I must have looked like a deer caught in the headlights because Margaret laughed her musical laugh and said, "Don't worry, Jennifer! This will be fun! You have all the words necessary in your head and in your heart. So let's begin!"

Margaret clapped her hands smartly together, and a loud *crack!* filled the air around us, accompanied by that same rumble of distant thunder. A mysterious door had just been flung open, and I knew then that I was about to embark on a miraculous journey with this special emissary from heaven.

Fearfully and Wonderfully Made

I have called you by name, you are mine.

Isaiah 43:1 (ESV)

As the thundering sounds slowly subsided into gentle echoes, Margaret looked over at me and grinned, showing all of her perfect white teeth. It did wonders to calm my pounding heart. Then without another word and to my great delight, Margaret raised her lovely hands toward the sky and began to recite a portion of one of my favorite psalms.

> For you created my inmost being; you knit me together in my mother's womb. I praise you because I am fearfully and wonderfully made; your works are wonderful, I know that full well. My frame was not hidden from you when I was made in the secret place. When I was woven together in the depths of the earth, your eyes

saw my unformed body. All the days ordained
for me were written in your book before one of
them came to be.

Psalm 139:13–16 (NIV)

Whoa! I thought. *Now, that is the way to begin a story!*
Bolstered by Margaret's presence and overwhelming
encouragement, I began to tell her my story. And I
started from the very beginning.

"In the wee hours of the morning on August 17,
1959, my mother, Sara, went into labor with me in
Detroit, Michigan. At that moment, some two hundred
miles away in Anderson, Indiana, my grandmother,
whom we called Nana, was awakened in her bedroom
by a voice exclaiming 'Mother!' Nana sat up, startled,
because the voice she heard sounded remarkably like
Sara calling out to her. She knew immediately that she
had to get on the train to make the journey to Detroit.
I have often wondered, was it an angel that spoke to
Nana as I was being born?"

I peered over at my new friend, hoping for an
answer, but Margaret only winked mysteriously and
nodded for me to continue.

"This strange and wonderful communication
happened at the very beginning of my life and has
occurred throughout my life with startling frequency.
This was the beginning of a journey that God had
planned out for me while I was but a twinkle in his
eye—a journey during which he has taught me my life's
greatest lesson: *to listen when he speaks.*

"My mother has a vivid memory that she has repeated to me on more than one occasion: I was not more than five years old, riding in the car with her. Sitting in the backseat, I let out one of my signature squeaky yawns—a yawn accompanied by a not-very-lady-like sound, like a door opening on creaky old hinges. My mother playfully exclaimed, 'Jennifer! What was that?' I replied very matter-of-factly, 'That was God talking!' If I had only known how prophetic that statement would be in my own life!"

Margaret suddenly burst out in a fit of giggles. "Oh, I'm so sorry for interrupting, Jennifer! That just reminded me of how often I heard that funny squeak coming from you at the most inopportune moments while you were growing up! Please keep going!" I rolled my eyes and laughed, a little embarrassed at the memory, and continued.

"Even as a very young child, I sensed that somehow, God could talk to people, and he was talking to me. This was the beginning of a lifetime of learning—learning to hear, to listen, to obey, and to discern the truths that he reveals in my dream visions. And, Margaret, at age fifty, I am *still* learning! I can tell you, God is an effective and persistent teacher!"

Margaret sighed softly and said, "It seems like just yesterday you were that sweet little girl with the squeaky yawn. And as young as you were, you were just beginning to sense a wonderful truth: *God speaks*.

"Let's pause here, Jenn, because I want to ask you a question. What do you suppose God was saying to you at such a very early stage in your life?"

I sat for a moment, reflecting on my distant memories…memories of the love of my parents and grandparents and the wide-eyed fascination I had with the world around me. Then I had my answer.

"Welcome to your life on earth, my precious little one. I have so much to share with you!"

Thirst

*As a deer longs for flowing streams, so my soul longs
for you, Oh God.*

My soul thirsts for God, for the living God.

Psalm 42:1–2 (NRSV)

Margaret reached over and gave my arm a playful
squeeze. "My rather sudden appearance here this
morning prevented you from having your morning
coffee, Jenn, which I know you dearly enjoy! Why don't
you go inside and pour yourself a cup? And while you
are at it, bring me one too!"

Her eyes sparkled in amusement as she witnessed
my astonished reaction. An angel that drinks coffee?
Now that, as a friend of mine would say, is way
groovy! I hurried inside and poured two fresh cups of
my favorite dark roast. Hannah and Isabel, my other
two dogs, followed me back outside. After giving our
angelic visitor curious sniffs and friendly tail wags, they
wandered off into the yard.

Margaret and I sat contentedly together, sipping our coffee and watching the morning backyard activity. Birds hopped from feeder to feeder, and a wary squirrel worked his way down the tree above the birdbath. Comically, he craned his neck to peek around the tree to see where the dogs were roaming in the yard. Confident that their backs were turned, he took his big chance and leapt the rest of the way onto the birdbath and took a long drink of water.

We burst out in a fit of giggles as we watched him finish up and leap back onto the tree, scampering high up into the branches, safe and sound.

"I am amazed, Margaret," I said, shaking my head, "at how these creatures have such good instincts. That little squirrel knew he needed water, knew where to find it, and also knew to avoid the danger that the three dogs posed to him."

"Where do you think that instinct comes from?" asked Margaret.

"Well, I don't know. I never really thought about it," I mused. "I guess it has just always been there."

"That instinct, Jennifer, is lovingly provided to each creature the moment God creates it so that it will have the knowledge it needs to survive. Humans are given that same gift. An instinct that leads them back to the Creator that loves and provides for them.

"You have sensed this instinct, or this connection, to your Creator in your own life, haven't you?" she asked knowingly.

"I have," I replied thoughtfully. "As a young girl, I sensed that I came from somewhere else even though my conscious mind did not remember where. It was a sense of belonging to something special much larger than myself—larger and, at the same time, intensely intimate and loving. I have never completely lost that sense of connection, though at times in my life, I have experienced what I would call momentary breaks, which have caused me great distress. Those episodes have taught me that this connection to God is what I need to survive.

"It makes sense to me that this instinct that you speak of, Margaret, may very well be the strong connection the soul has to its Creator, and when this connection somehow breaks through to the human consciousness, it creates the desire in the hearts of men and women to seek a relationship with God."

Margaret nodded and gave me a gentle smile. "The scripture that says *my soul thirsts for God* is a beautiful way to describe this desire to connect with your Creator. In my experience, when people begin to ask the questions '*who am I?*' and '*what is my purpose here?*' they are beginning to *thirst*, to sense a connection to something greater than themselves. Do you want to know a secret, dear one?" I nodded as I listened intently to her. "They are beginning to sense their heavenly origin!"

I suddenly recalled a statement by St. Augustine that I read some time ago and shared it with Margaret:

> Why do we not know the country whose citizens we are? Because we have wandered so far away that we have forgotten it. But the Lord Christ, the king of the land, came down to us,

and drove forgetfulness from our hearts. God took to Himself our flesh so that He might be our way back.

"I love this quote, Margaret, because I really like the idea of being a 'citizen of heaven' first and a citizen of earth second!"

Margaret laughed softly. "Well, as a citizen of heaven, my dear child, I certainly can understand why that would be an appealing thought! You know, young children have some of the best testimonies about their heavenly citizenship, because many retain their memories of heaven for a short time during childhood."

Margaret's words triggered another memory that I related to her. "Several years ago, I read a book called *The Soul's Remembrance: Earth is not our Home*, by Roy Mills. He defines the soul's remembrance as 'the ability to remember Heaven and never lose contact with it.' He writes that his gift from God was to be able to retain his memories of heaven throughout his life. Roy's memories are astounding. He never spoke about his gift or his memories of heaven until God prompted him to write a book about it later on in life.

"In Dr. Elisabeth Kubler-Ross's enthusiastic review of Roy's book, she wrote, 'I have interviewed thousands of young children before they go to school and many know where they came from…We have learned much about death, but the spiritual origin of man…where we come from before birth…that, my friends, is the next great area of research.'"

I paused a moment to take a long, slow sip of coffee and to let these last thoughts sink in. It is thrilling to know that our humble existence here on earth is in fact only part of a much more expansive existence. Oh, how I wish I could have retained my memories of heaven!

"Jennifer," Margaret said quietly, startling me out of my thoughts, "do you see those three sweet little blonde heads popping up over the fence in the back of your yard?"

I looked way to the back of the acre-deep yard where she was pointing, and sure enough, three little blonde heads bobbed up and down. I could just barely hear their squeals of delight as these children jumped on their backyard trampoline.

Margaret smiled, watching them, and whispered, "Why, even the hairs of your head are all numbered" (Luke 12:7 ESV).

I looked over at Margaret, a puzzled expression on my face.

"Dear one," she replied softly, "our Father in heaven loves each of his children so very much. And yes, he knows you so intimately that he has even counted the hairs on your head. Every single person who has walked this earth began their journey in heaven, and each of you has been lovingly and joyfully bounced on our Father's knee. Before he sent you into this world, he whispered something special into your ear, something meant for you and you alone. Even though a veil has been placed over your conscious memory of heaven, your soul remembers God's special whisper. That memory may very well be what you experienced as a young girl when you felt that connection to something intimate and loving."

"Oh, Margaret, that is beautiful!" I exclaimed, goose bumps forming up and down my arms. "When you put it that way, it sounds as if God began talking to us even *before* we were born!"

"Oh, he did indeed." Margaret smiled knowingly. "Listen, Jenn, to what God told the prophet Jeremiah when he called him into service: 'Before I formed you in the womb I knew you, and before you were born I consecrated you; I appointed you a prophet to the nations' (Jeremiah 1:5 ESV)."

Margaret's eyes twinkled as she watched a dawning amazement creep across my face as I absorbed these words and the truth behind them. Then my angel friend stood and gracefully brushed the folds from her gown. "Let's take a break here for a moment, Jennifer. I want to pour myself another cup of your delicious coffee. I will bring one for you too. Sit here, and while you wait, I want you to think of the message that God had for you during this time of awakening in your young life. I'll be right back!"

When Margaret returned, I had an answer for her.

"Remember my whisper. You have been mine from the beginning."

Heart's Delight

Be still and know that I am God.

Psalm 46:10 (ESV)

Margaret placed our coffee on the table and then wandered over to peruse my rose and herb gardens. I remained seated, closed my eyes, and tilted my face to the warm sun, willing my senses to absorb whatever this blessed morning had to offer. I heard the trickle of the pool waterfall, the occasional giggle of delight from the trampolining children, and the gentle tinkle of wind chimes in the breeze. A blooming sweet almond tree scented the air with its thick perfume. Moments like this are so precious, kind of like a spa moment for the soul.

After several minutes, Margaret rejoined me at the table. "Your garden smells wonderful!" she exclaimed. "Especially the rosemary!"

"You should smell it after it rains, my friend," I replied. "It is *heavenly!*"

"Mmm." Margaret nodded, sniffing the air again. "Our Lord gives us such special little gifts every day, gifts for all of the senses!

"This brings me to my next question for you, Jenn. Earlier, you described to me how as a young child you sensed the presence of God. Now, I want you to tell me in what ways you *experienced* his presence. This is important because your connection to God goes back to the days and experiences of your childhood, in ways you may have been completely unaware. You may need to take a few minutes to think about this."

She was right. I sat with my eyes closed and returned to the days of my youth. I had such a wonderful childhood, with so many varied experiences. How was I going to find the ones that Margaret was referring to? Then a thought came to me. When did I experience a quickening in my heart, a stirring in my soul that I could *feel*?

Amazingly, one by one, the memories tumbled in.

"Hmmm," I began thoughtfully, "I think the first way I remember experiencing God's presence was while I was being still—a very hard thing for a busy, talkative little girl to be!"

Margaret snickered again and covered her mouth quickly with her hands, nodding for me to keep going. Okay, I admit, talkative was probably an understatement—and still is!

"As a young girl, the times I experienced God's presence was whenever I felt an unbidden stirring of my heart. For instance, I experienced sensations of *holiness* as I gazed up at the stained glass window in church of Jesus kneeling in prayer; *ancient,* as I lay on the sand and looked up at the night sky filled with stars over Lake Michigan; *wonder,* as I sat in rapt attention listening to a Christmas Eve story about a donkey and other stable animals kneeling at Mary's feet the moment Jesus was born; *calm,* as I put my toes in the water as it lapped softly on the sandy shore of Lake Erie; *contentment,* as I witnessed the love my parents had for each other; *beauty,* as I closed my eyes and immersed myself in the sounds and music of the cello; *love,* as I arrived home from school and was met at the door by the smell of freshly baked chocolate chip cookies; *peace,* as I walked alone on a frigid, moonlit night, snow crunching under my boots and stars twinkling above bright and clear; *anticipation,* as I awakened on Easter Sunday morning; *delight,* as our caroling group quietly gathered to sing 'Silent Night' at an unsuspecting neighbor's door while candle wax melted all over my mittens; *awe,* as I stood on the shore of the ocean, water stretching as far as the eye could see; and *joy,* upon witnessing a rainbow.

"Each of these experiences, Margaret, involved the use of one or more of my senses and, for the most part, occurred while I was being *quiet* or *still.*"

"You are right, dear one," Margaret affirmed. "The easiest place to find God is in the quiet. It is where you can experience him with all of your senses since they are not occupied by other things."

"Speaking of senses, Margaret, there is another powerful way I have experienced God as a young girl and throughout my life. I'm sure you know all about this, my angel friend," I teased.

Margaret clapped her hands and joyfully exclaimed, "*Music!*"

"You guessed right!" I responded. "Music is and always has been one of the primary ways I experience God's presence. Through the beauty of an orchestra, the words of a hymn, the blend of choral voices, the majesty of a pipe organ… The list could go on and on.

"I have often wondered how human beings even came up with the idea of music. From the beginning of time, we have somehow found ways to create lovely, meaningful sounds, *music*, to express our emotions, to celebrate, to mourn. So couldn't it be possible that our souls have already experienced the beautiful music of heaven, and as human beings, we are constantly trying to recreate what our souls remember—the glorious praise music of heaven's angels?"

I looked over at Margaret for affirmation. She was positively quivering in her seat, and I knew that this was a subject very dear to her own heart. She did not offer a comment, so I continued.

"I have a particularly poignant memory of sitting on my daddy's lap by the fire on a cold winter evening, listening to one of his favorite operas, *La Boheme*. It was early in my childhood. I could not have been more than six years old, and it was my first memory of listening to opera. It was so intensely beautiful. As Daddy told me the story of Mimi, her love story, and her eventual tragic death from tuberculosis, I vividly remember being filled with a multitude of emotions as the music and story unfolded. Tears streamed down my cheeks as Mimi drew her last breath and the love of her life cried out for her. My young soul was flooded with feelings way beyond my years, emotions I did not yet understand, yet they were real. It astounded me that I could be so moved by music."

I paused for a moment as I heard a soft sigh. I looked at Margaret, and a small tear was running down her cheek. I knew then that she remembered this precious evening just as fondly as I did.

"A few years ago, I heard a wonderful true story about the music of heaven. Reverend Don Piper came to talk to our former church about his book *90 Minutes in Heaven*. During his talk, Rev. Piper recalled his fatal accident on a Texas road that left him declared dead by paramedics. His body sat for ninety minutes awaiting removal from the scene. Don told us that during this interval, he entered heaven and remembers experiencing the most beautiful music he had ever heard. He described it as beautiful, continuous worship melodies that completely filled and surrounded him. Don emotionally remarked that this music filled his heart with the deepest joy he had ever experienced."

"Oh, darling girl, Reverend Piper is so right!" exclaimed my angel friend. She jumped out of her chair, no longer able to contain her enthusiasm. "The music of heaven is so *glorious*! One day, Jenn, you will hear the music again with heavenly ears—nothing on earth can compare! Oh, how I wish I was back before the throne singing praises to our Lord *right now!*" She clapped her hands and laughed joyfully. Then she stopped and looked at me with a sheepish grin. "Oops, got a little carried away. Sorry! Please continue." She sat back down and folded her hands primly before her.

"No problem." I laughed. "Actually, what you just said reminds me of scriptures I have read that refer to the music of heaven. In the book of Revelation, the apostle John vividly describes his visions of the music of heaven. In chapter fifteen verses two and three, he sees believers holding harps and singing, and in chapter five verse thirteen, he hears all creatures in heaven and earth singing praises to the glory of God.

"Several years ago, I came across a fascinating description of the origin of music in a collection of mid-1700's writings by Emanuel Swedenborg called the *Arcana Coelestia 8337*. In it, he presents a case for the spiritual origin of music: 'In former times, many types of musical instruments were used when God was worshipped, but with much discrimination. In general, wind instruments were used to express affections (emotions) for good, and stringed instruments affections for truth; and the origin of this was the correspondence of every sound to the affections.'

"This statement goes on to say that 'It is well-known that some types of musical instruments are used to express one kind of natural affections and other types to express another kind, and that when a fitting melody is played they actually stir the affections. Skilled musicians know all about this and also make proper use of it. The reason for it lies in the very nature of sound, and its accord with the affections. Mankind at first learned about it not from science and art but through the ear and its keen sense of hearing. From this it is plain that the ability does not have its origin in the natural world but in the spiritual world.'"

Poor Margaret just could not contain herself any longer. She jumped out of her chair, her face radiant, and raised her arms to the sky. With a clear voice that could only belong to an angel, she began singing a psalm of praise. "Make a joyful noise to the Lord, all the Earth! Serve the Lord with gladness! Come into his presence with singing!

"Oh, my child, what a blessed gift our Lord has given his children to carry with them to this world from the realm of heaven!"

Overcome with emotion, I could only say "Amen!"

Margaret returned to her chair and we sat in silence for several minutes until both of us could get our emotions in check. Then, in a quiet voice, she asked, "What did you hear God saying to you, Jennifer, as you experienced his presence with all of your senses during your childhood?"

My answer rose like a song in my heart.

"I am here, dear one, in everything that is beautiful to you. Look for me in all that you love."

Lord, Hear My Prayer

*Rejoice in the Lord always; again I will say,
Rejoice. Let your gentleness be known to everyone.
The Lord is near. Do not worry about anything,
but in everything by prayer and supplication with
thanksgiving, let your requests be made known
to God. And the peace of God, which surpasses all
understanding, will guard your hearts and your
minds in Christ Jesus.*

Philippians 4:4–7 (NRSV)

My normal morning routine included a fair amount of
exercise or activity, and this morning's events had blown
"normal" right out the window. Our conversations in
the garden had been so riveting that I had not noticed
my lack of activity until I shifted in my chair and felt
a twinge of stiffness. I rose and walked to the edge of
the patio and indulged in a long, luxurious stretch,
and oh, it felt good! I looked through my fingertips as
they reached toward the sky and marveled at the view
that was revealed through the treetops. The sky was a

pristine cerulean blue, and the green leaves of the trees glistened with a silver reflection of the brilliant sun.

I have come to think of these trees as my gentle giants, reaching their branches high up into the sky. As a breeze rustled through the treetops, these giants swayed gently back and forth, and I was moved by how they looked as if they were raising their great arms in prayer. Their movements made a whispering sound, like the exhalation of a long, soft sigh. I wondered what prayers or praises they were offering to their Creator. Maybe they were thanking God for another day of life in this beautiful world.

Margaret joined me and matched the direction of her gaze with mine. "Wonderful, isn't it, Jenn? Even these great trees joyfully communicate with their Maker."

Startled, I looked at her sharply. She seemed to know what I had been thinking!

Margaret laughed. "All of creation speaks to God. And you, child, are no exception. As you have just described, you *sensed* God's presence and *experienced* his presence as a young girl. And as I watched you grow up, I was overjoyed to observe you seek God in a new way. You began to *speak* to him.

"Before you tell me about that part of your life, would you join hands with me for a quick prayer?" She held out both hands to me.

Silently, I nodded and took her hands in mine. I closed my eyes and waited for her to begin. The breeze swirled playfully around us, and again I detected the faint scent of roses.

In her clear voice, Margaret prayed, "God, come close. Come quickly! Open your ears—it's my voice you're hearing! Treat my prayer as sweet incense rising; my raised hands are my evening prayers."

"Oh, Margaret! That was beautiful! " I exclaimed, touched by these sweet words.

"It *is* beautiful, Jenn! It is the beginning of *The Message's* translation of Psalm 141, a prayer written by our beloved King David. I thought it fitting for this next part of your story, which I want to hear about as soon as we sit back down."

I thought to myself, *I wonder if Margaret knows King David? Wouldn't it be amazing to sit at his feet and listen to his wonderful prayers!*

As soon as we settled into our chairs, I enthusiastically began to tell my friend about how I began to speak to God. This is a story I love to tell!

"I have always been a voracious reader, and one day in my early teens, I stumbled upon a magazine article written by the Reverend Billy Graham about prayer. His article talked about how important prayer is in the lives of God's people and that prayer needs to be an ongoing dialogue between you and God. I was riveted by this statement. Prayer was something that I did before going to bed, and my prayers were not very personal or sophisticated. They pretty much consisted of 'now I lay me down to sleep' with a few thank-you's and blessings mixed in. And admittedly, many nights I just plain forgot to say my prayers.

"As I read, I thought to myself, *An ongoing dialogue? Would God listen to me if I talked to him during the day?*"

I paused for a moment and gazed at Margaret. She was nodding her head vigorously up and down, trying very hard not to say a word.

"Reverend Graham's article really bothered me because I felt that maybe God wanted me to be communicating with him more, and I was not doing what he wanted. And I could not pray in the beautiful prayer language that our minister used in church. My prayers sounded childlike compared to his. How could I talk with God, the Creator of the Universe, the great I AM, without being able to use the grown-up, flowery language of prayer I was used to hearing? After contemplating this for a day or so, I got out pen and paper and proceeded to write a letter to Reverend Graham. The magazine had published his organization's address at the end of the article.

"My letter was very straightforward. I asked Reverend Graham how to pray so that God would listen to me. I mailed my letter with a great sense of anticipation, and then I waited…and waited.

"Time passed, and I completely forgot about my letter. My teenage girl mind was otherwise occupied by boys and music heartthrobs David Cassidy, Donny Osmond, and Bobby Sherman. Then one day, my mother walked into my bedroom with a rather amazed look on her face. She was carrying an envelope, and said, 'Jennifer, you have a letter from Billy Graham!'

"Wow! I did indeed have a response from Reverend Graham, and for me, it was profound. He thanked me for my letter and for my thoughtful question. In his response, he explained that prayer was something everyone can do, children and adults alike. 'All you have to do,' he wrote, 'is to talk to God like he is your friend. Just tell him whatever is in your heart. Don't worry about using fancy words. He loves you and wants to hear from you.' I asked myself, *Could it really be that simple?*

"It took some practice, mostly to *remember* to pray, but I began that very day talking to God as if he were my friend. And I discovered that Reverend Graham's advice really *was* simple. I gave God thanks for the things I had, the people I loved, and asked him for help with the problems I had, some silly school stuff, and some not so silly stuff.

"When I was fourteen, my grandfather, a physician, noticed a lump in my neck and talked to my father, also a physician, about it. I ended up seeing a surgeon who recommended surgery 'because it may be cancer.' My mother had recently lost her best friend to breast cancer, so the word *cancer* and the thought of possibly having it, scared the living daylights out of me. I was so glad to be able to talk to God about it, and I did a lot. The night before I had to go to the hospital, I lay in my pretty little twin bed and prayed. I was really scared, and yet a wonderful peace came over me while I prayed. It felt as if someone had their arms around me, and I knew that I would be okay, no matter what the outcome was. I was actually able to go to sleep that night. The surgery went on as scheduled, and I had a benign growth on my thyroid gland, which was removed. No cancer.

"What helped me the most was being able to talk to God through the whole process, and I began to have an assurance that he was listening. I owe my heartfelt thanks to Reverend Graham for taking the time to answer a young girl's question. It made a monumental difference in my life. Once I had learned how to pray with the assurance that God was listening to *me*, I would be ready to learn *two-way* communication with the Almighty—to learn how to listen to *him*."

Margaret sat very still for a moment and then looked at me, her blue eyes misting with tears. "You were very fortunate indeed, Jennifer, to have had the guidance of Billy Graham. He has been responsible for leading hundreds of thousands of souls to the throne of our precious Lord. He has used his anointing well. And, child, no one knows better than our Lord the value of prayer. While he was here on earth, he relied on prayer to keep in constant touch with his Heavenly Father.

"So, my dear girl, you have begun to talk to our Father in heaven with heartfelt innocence and expectation. What do you feel God's message was for you as you entered into a prayerful relationship with him?"

I smiled as I thought about the precious prayer times I share with God and answered,

"I love to hear from you, my beloved child. I am always listening, hoping to hear your sweet voice. From your lips to my heart."

A wistful sigh escaped Margaret's lips as she said, "Oh, dear one, how I wish all of God's children knew how dearly he wants to hear from them each day. His heart longs to hear from his beloved, no matter what time of the day or night."

Margaret smiled at me, and as she did, I began to detect the scent of white roses in the air again.

"I am going to leave you for a while and let you get on with your day, Jennifer. After all, it is your birthday! Have a wonderful day, and I will return here at sunset. Will you meet me out here then?"

"Of course, I will," I replied, disappointment seeping into my heart. I had really been enjoying this extraordinary morning with my special angel.

Margaret sensed my disappointment and gave me an amused giggle. "Oh my, don't worry, Jenn. I am not nearly through with you yet! We have much, much more to discuss. Until tonight, then!" She blew me a kiss and walked out into the backyard, her gown shimmering until she disappeared into thin air.

Ask, Seek, Knock

*And I tell you, ask and it will be given to you; seek, and
you will find; knock, and it will will be opened to you.
For everyone who asks receives, and the one who seeks
finds, and to the one who knocks it will be opened.*

Luke 11:9–10 (ESV)

After an afternoon filled with shopping, lunch, and
laughter with girlfriends, I eagerly counted the minutes
until the arrival of sunset, when my angel was to return.
At the appointed hour, I walked out onto the patio. No
Margaret, yet. It was still quite warm, so I sat down at
the pool's edge and dangled my bare legs in the cool
water. Slowly moving my legs back and forth, creating
big swirls in the water, I thought about my morning
conversations with Margaret. As my wise angel friend
led me systematically through the ways I experienced
God during the various stages of my young life, it had
become evident that he has been a consistent part of
my life since before I was born. What a delicious truth!

I began to see reflections of orange and pink in the
swirls of blue water, and I lifted my face to the sky.

Tonight's sunset was breathtaking. Huge streaks of brilliant, fiery orange and pink raced across the sky as if they had been finger-painted on a vast canvas with a giant hand. The lovely view brought to mind a saying I had heard somewhere before. It said, "The sunrise is God's greeting, and the sunset is his signature." I closed my eyes and whispered a prayer of thanks for such a beautiful signature to the end of a very special birthday.

A sudden movement in the air next to me caused my eyes to snap open. There was my lovely Margaret, sitting next to me, dangling her legs in the water next to mine!

"A beautiful sunset, isn't it, Jenn?"

I nodded with a grin, my heart thrilled at her return.

We sat together, watching the colors of the sky deepen, adding hues of lavender and purple. The soft swirls of water reflected pink, orange, blue, lavender, and purple, mixing gently like an artist's watercolor palette.

"I couldn't think of a more beautiful ending to today," I said with a quiet sigh. "God truly has had his hand on this day, from beginning to end. It began with a house filled with the scent of white roses, then your miraculous appearance, and now it ends with this gorgeous sunset."

"Mm…" Margaret replied, nodding in blissful agreement. She leaned down, scooped up a handful of water, and let it trickle back into the pool through her fingers. With astonishment, I watched as her whole body began to shimmer and glow with a soft light. The large drops that fell from her fingers formed ever-expanding rings in the water, which also began to shimmer with this mysterious luminescence.

Margaret looked at me and said tenderly, "Jesus said, 'Those who drink the water I give will never be thirsty again. It becomes a fresh, bubbling spring within them, giving them eternal life' (John 4:14 NLT).

"I was a witness, dear child, as you made the most important decision of your young life and jumped heart first into the waters of eternal life. Our Heavenly Prince remembers so fondly the moment you opened your heart and your life to him and the joy it brought to all of us in heaven! He would like for you to share that story with me now."

I felt a thrill of excitement run up and down my spine. I couldn't think of a better ending to this precious day than to tell my angel friend about the events that led to that day long ago, when my heart was changed forever.

"When I was in the eighth grade, my family attended the beautiful Old Stone Church in Cleveland, Ohio. That year, I enrolled in Communicant's class, which prepared young people to officially join the church, declare Christ as Savior, and receive communion at a ceremony held on Maundy Thursday. Our minister was a fiery redhead—a former Canadian fisherman, if my memory serves me correctly—and oh, could he preach! He had a deep love for the Lord, and you could feel his passion in his sermons. I often sat listening to him and thought that it would be so nice to have such a passion for God, but it just was not there for me yet. Pleasant and lovely feelings, yes, but *passion*? No.

"I completed my Communicant's curriculum with my fellow classmates and was formally initiated into the church on March 30, 1973. I still have the little white Bible that was presented to me by a dear family friend on that special day. Being able to take communion with my parents and all of the adult church members from that day forward was a great privilege. But something still seemed to be missing. I just wasn't feeling the passion I had expected. When I heard people speak of their personal relationships with Christ, I kind of scratched my head. Huh? *Personal* relationship? I just didn't get it!"

At this, a very un-angel-like snort erupted beside me. I looked over to see Margaret again with both hands pressed firmly over her mouth, lest she dare let out any more sounds. Her eyes were squinched tightly shut and her shoulders bobbed up and down.

Good grief! I sighed to myself. She obviously knows me pretty well since there are lots of times I just don't get it. My husband derives much amusement in hearing me say "I don't get it!" after a joke he has just told.

"Hey, Margaret," I said to her, "a little support here, please! I am getting to the part where I finally get it!"

"So sorry!" she said in a quivering voice, obviously still trying to reign in her glee. "Please continue!"

"Okay. Let's fast-forward to the summer of 1974, when my family traveled to our annual vacation destination in Traverse City, Michigan. My father shut down his busy medical practice for two weeks, and he and my mother packed our family and supplies into the station wagon and made the eight-hour drive to our log cabin on the bay of Lake Michigan. Oh, how we all loved it there! Sandy beaches; pine forests; beautiful, cold, clear water; a raft to swim out to…and our cousins! My aunt Adrienne and uncle Don and their family traveled to Traverse City from Indiana every year at the same time for a three-week stay. It was such fun to have this time to be all together. This particular year, things were a little different. As our two weeks came to a close, one of my older teenage cousins wanted to go home with my family to take in some Cleveland Indians baseball games, and I wanted to stay an extra week at the beach. So we worked out a trade. My cousin would go to Cleveland, and I would stay with Adrienne and Don and family for an extra week, and then we would make a kid exchange somewhere in between Ohio and Indiana.

"My aunt and uncle were accomplished sailors and had their red-and-white sailboat with them. Every day during that extra week, they took me sailing out on the bay. I remember being very afraid of the deep blue water, which I knew was way over my head. Uncle Don, formerly an engineer, had responded to God's calling in his life and had become pastor of an Indiana church. While we sailed in the deep blue waters, he told me a story from the Bible about Jesus in the boat with his disciples, who were also afraid. He told me about how Jesus calmed them and calmed the storm. I learned a lot about Jesus in the days that followed. So much so that I felt my heart changing, kind of like how in Dr. Seuss's *How the Grinch Stole Christmas*, the Grinch's heart grew three sizes bigger in one day! My little white Bible was filling up with notes and underlined scriptures. I could not get enough of this wonderful Jesus, who, really, if it could be possible, wanted to be my *friend*! I quite literally was falling in love with him. By the end of the week, I asked how I could go about receiving Jesus as my personal Savior, since I took seriously his promise in Luke 11:9–10. With great joy, my aunt and uncle knelt with me at the bedside in prayer, and I prayed six simple words: *'Jesus, please come into my life!'*

"Guess what, Margaret," I teased, "I finally *got* it!"

She beamed her beautiful smile at me. "You sure did! And you should have seen the celebration in heaven when you spoke those precious words. 'For there is joy before the angels of God over one sinner who repents'" (Luke 15:10 ESV).

Just the thought of angels rejoicing for little ol' me still makes my heart leap! I continued with my story.

"The first thing that happened after I spoke those six words was that I saw another word form in my mind. It was *kham*. I was puzzled and asked my aunt and uncle what that meant. They answered simply, 'Just say it.' So I said it, and oh my goodness! Words of a language unknown to me came pouring forth from my mouth. It went on and on, and the most incredible joy was bubbling up inside me so fast that I couldn't hold it inside anymore. I burst out laughing, and my aunt and uncle did too. This was my first gift of the Spirit. It was completely unexpected, and a bit puzzling, since I could not understand any of the words. But through the years, I have come to understand this gift and what it means to me, and it is one of my most treasured gifts."

"Let me interject something here, Jennifer," interrupted Margaret. "This first gift of the Spirit God gave you is quite real, and I know that you have come across people in your life who have made you feel uncomfortable about it. God has a purpose for every gift he gives you, and he expects you to find ways to use your gifts that will glorify him and lead others to him. I hope that you will have something more to say about this later on!"

Margaret was right. I do have more to say on the subject. But later, because there is still much to tell, so I continued on with my story.

"When I returned home to my family, I needed some time to come down from my 'mountaintop experience'—to get my elation and exuberance for the Lord to a manageable state. I think I drove everyone a little crazy for a bit. But I finally settled down and got busy with school and all the things that go along with being a flaky teenage girl. There was something different about me, though. Because now, I knew in my heart that Jesus was my wonderful friend and that, no matter what I was feeling, I could talk to him. For me, that was huge. I particularly recall one day in dance class. I was auditioning for a dance team and had to complete several moves that did not come easily to me. Much to my chagrin, I was not the most graceful dancer."

I shot Margaret a look before she could erupt in another snort. "No comments, please, from the peanut gallery!" I playfully commanded. "I am freely admitting my klutziness!" She just nodded and pressed her lips together tightly to suppress what I had rightly suspected was going to erupt.

"So when it was my turn to do a dance walk across the balance beam, I knew I was in big trouble. I never could do it in practice without falling off the beam. As it got closer to my turn, I breathed a quick prayer, asking Jesus to help me with this. I stepped onto the beam and began dance-stepping across. Then the most amazing thing happened! I felt someone holding my hand! *Really, truly, holding my hand!* I danced across that beam flawlessly! I *know* Jesus was there holding my hand that day. I made the dance team, as an apprentice, but I made it!

"This was an important time of awakening in my life. I knew that with all of my flaws, God loved me and was truly there for me. I was gaining assurance that when I prayed, he was listening. I began to have confidence in my relationship with the Almighty, and my heart was filled with love for him. The passion that I had longed for was finally inside of me. I could now truly take the words of Deuteronomy 6:5 into my heart and live them: 'You shall love the Lord your God with all your heart and with all your mind and with all your might'" (ESV).

Margaret's eyes were filled with happy tears as I finished my story. She dipped her hands in the water again and took both of my hands in hers. "So, precious child, what was the message our Lord Jesus had for you when you knelt at that bedside and jumped head and heart first into the waters of his promise of eternal life?"

I looked down at my hands, bathed in the still luminescent water that Margaret had scooped from the pool. My heart felt as if it would burst from joy as I gave her my answer:

"I am yours forever, my beloved, for you are now baptized in me. I can't wait to explore our future together."

The stage was set. A relationship had begun. It was now time for me to begin learning.

Dream Girl

I slept, but my heart was awake.

Song of Solomon 5:2 (ESV)

The next morning dawned warm and humid. By 8:30 a.m. it was already eighty degrees. I fidgeted around the house, trying to keep my eyes off the clock, awaiting Margaret's return. She left me just after sunset the night before and had promised an early-morning appearance.

Suddenly, as I passed by the kitchen window with a large load of laundry in my arms, I again saw a shimmer of light in the garden. I hurried into the laundry room, threw the pile on the floor, and ran outside, holding my breath and pleading silently, *Please, oh, please, let that be my Margaret!*

Sure enough, there she was, standing beside the pool where we sat last evening, a vision of loveliness. Today her sparkling gown was a pale buttercup yellow.

"Good morning to you, Jennifer!" She beamed with a smile that reflected the light of heaven.

I practically ran over to join her. I was astounded at how much I loved this angel I had just met.

We stood together on the patio, watching God's creatures celebrate the beginning of the new day. Birds, butterflies, and squirrels flitted and jumped and played among the trees and flower beds. Margaret spied my statue of St. Francis of Assisi in one of my garden beds, appropriately named by my daddy as the Assisi Garden. She walked over to get a closer look, and I followed.

"A nice choice for your backyard, Jennifer. Did you know that Francis called the birds and animals of the earth his brothers and sisters?"

"Yes, as a matter of fact, that is one of the reasons I have always felt so close to Francis, because birds and animals are so close to my own heart. St. Francis has popped up in my life so many times in art, literature, and nature that I just had to put him in my garden."

Margaret continued on, walking deeper into the yard, and as she stepped from the shadows of the trees into the sunlight, the most remarkable sight met my eyes. I saw the faintest glimmer behind her shoulders. Was it… I did a double take and squinted hard, trying to make out what I was seeing. Again, a glimmer, a shimmer…an outline of *wings*! Huge, head-to-toe, *beautiful, transparent wings*! "Margaret!" I exclaimed. "I didn't know you had wings. They are beautiful! Have you had those all along?"

"Why yes," she replied. "I just chose this time to reveal them to you. In a way, you are about to talk about this very thing when you begin to share what God has revealed to you in your life. Just like not being able to see my wings until I stepped into the light, your eyes and heart did not see God's deeper truths until he chose a time to reveal them to you. And what our Father reveals is always good, always true, and holds many wonders even if we don't understand right away. As I walk back into the shadows, you will no longer see my wings, but they are still there. God's truth is also always there. It was there at the very beginning and will be there for eternity. To see it, all we need to do is look into the Light, the Light of the World."

I nodded and blinked back tears, having nothing coherent to say at the moment.

She smiled in understanding, and her blue eyes crinkled up at the edges.

"In your story, we have come to the stage in your life when new and important gifts are emerging. I want you to speak of these new gifts in a moment when we sit down. Walk with me and listen to these words from scripture: The second chapter of Daniel verse twenty-eight says, 'There is a God in heaven who reveals mysteries. Your dream and the visions of your head as you lay in bed are these.' And in Jeremiah 33:3 the Lord tells Jeremiah, 'Call to me and I will answer you, and will tell you great and hidden things that you have not known.'"

As we began walking back to the table together, I admit I was still preoccupied by the revelation of Margaret's wings. But the scriptures that Margaret quoted were so strikingly appropriate to my own life's experience that, as we settled comfortably in our chairs, I was anxious to continue with my story.

"God does not waste time in using the gifts he bestows upon us. Shortly after I began my personal relationship with Christ, I began to dream. Not just any dreams, but dreams that left me with feelings of concern, amazement, and quite honestly, a healthy dose of fear. But all had one common denominator—I was being given information about current or future events that no one else knew. These dreams began as secular, of this world and everyday life, and later moved to include deep sacred, or spiritual, truths."

Nana's Injury

The first dream was about my Nana. I dreamed that she was walking out of an office building and descending a set of stairs. Halfway down the stairs, she tripped and fell, rolled down the remaining steps and landed at the bottom, her back broken. When I awakened, I was so relieved to realize that this had been only a dream!

However, my elation did not last long. I cannot recall the time of year this was, but I do remember that my family was sitting down in the dining room having breakfast together later that morning, so it must have been a weekend or holiday. The telephone rang while we were eating, and my mother got up from the table to answer it. She came back a little while later with a stricken look on her face. She said, *"Nana fell and broke her back."*

Sitting in my seat, I felt the floor rushing up to meet me and a ringing in my ears. I was so shocked that

I nearly fainted. I wondered with dread if I caused this because I dreamed it. As it turned out, she did not fall exactly as I saw it in my dream—she fell at home. But the fact remained that I knew it before anyone else did. I don't believe I mentioned this to anyone because I was terrified. Thankfully, Nana recovered and my dreams returned to their normal harmless wackiness. What was very unsettling to me, though, was that *my prayers to Jesus about this incident were met with silence.*

Doomed Flight?

The summer of my twentieth birthday, I had the opportunity to go to England and Scotland as a chaperone for a high school marching band. The school was my alma mater, and my sister marched with the band as a flag carrier. The band was making a trip from Cleveland, Ohio, to the town of Redcar in Cleveland County, England. My father was accompanying the band as the attending physician, and my mother as another chaperone. We were all so excited as the date for our departure in June approached. As excited as I was, I was also experiencing a strange and unusual dread. I had numerous dreams of problems with the airplane on our trip. I loved to fly and had never experienced a flight with problems. I chalked this up to nerves and excitement, but as the date drew closer, my dread increased to the point I almost told my parents that I did not want to go on the trip. After telling myself a thousand times that I was just being silly, the date arrived. We went to the airport and boarded our plane from Cleveland to Boston. And the flight went off without a hitch! We arrived in Boston and walked to the gate to board our next plane, which would take us across the Atlantic to Glasgow, Scotland. When we got to the gate, I could hardly believe my eyes. There in the window was the giant nose of the biggest plane I had ever seen! It was a Boeing 747.

The plane loaded, doors closed, and we were off. There were two aisles and three sections of seats—one on each side and one in the middle. I sat in the middle section ahead of the wings next to my father on one side and a rather obnoxious teenage boy who was a drummer with the marching band and, to my chagrin, kept playing imaginary drums on his tray table. Not fifteen minutes into the flight, there was a large *bang!* and the plane veered on its right side, then veered on its left side, then straightened out. "Cool!" exclaimed drummer boy next to me. *Not* cool, I thought. I had flown enough to know that was not normal. A minute later, a flight attendant approached my father and quietly requested his presence in the back of the plane. He got up and went with her. Then the pilot's voice came over the com system: "Ladies and gentlemen, we have experienced a problem, and one of our four engines is damaged. The engine caught fire, and the fire has been extinguished. We could make it across the ocean with the remaining three engines, but for safety's sake, we have decided to return to Boston. The problem is that we have a full fuel tank and are too heavy to land, so we are going to have to circle and dump fuel until we are light enough to turn around and land back in Boston." My father came back and told us that a woman in the back had become hysterical because she was sitting behind the wing and saw the engine catch fire. *Great*. My thoughts quickly returned to the feelings of dread and the dreams of problems with the airplane that I had been experiencing during the prior months. What was God trying to tell me? Had he really wanted me to cancel my flight? Or as I was beginning to suspect, was there another message hidden in all this?

It took about twenty minutes of circling and dumping fuel before we could attempt a landing in Boston. It was a helpless feeling to be in the air for those twenty minutes knowing there was a serious problem with the plane, and I said a lot of prayers. This was an emergency landing, and as the plane neared the runway, we could see fire trucks lining both sides of the runway. Our landing was uneventful, no more fire. The airline did not have another plane available in Boston for us, so they had to have another 747 flown in from LaGuardia in New York. In the meantime, they would not let us exit the damaged plane, so they served us a meal while we waited. I remember feeling desperate to get off that plane. As soon as the new 747 arrived and we had boarded it, the dread I had been feeling for so long instantly vanished! I knew that this next flight would be a breeze, and it was. An interesting sideline to this story is that my mother had also been having the same dread and reservations about flying on this trip that I had, and neither of us had voiced our feelings.

This was a lesson to me to begin to pay attention to the warnings in my dreams.

A Baby's Heart

In the mid-1980s, I was living in Cleveland, Ohio. Friends of mine, whom I had not seen in several years, were expecting their first child. During the eighth month of my friend's pregnancy, I dreamed that there was a serious problem with the baby's heart, and that the baby may die. It was a very disturbing dream and kind of strange because I had not been in touch with her lately. I wondered why on earth I would be dreaming about her baby. My previous experiences with dreams that came true made me think twice about this one. What was I supposed to do? Call a friend that I cared deeply for yet had not seen in a long time, a very pregnant friend, and tell her something is wrong with her baby? I think not! Again, I let this go, telling myself that, for the most part, my dreams are just dreams and do not come true.

The baby's due date finally arrived, and my friends were blessed with a baby boy. But immediately, things went terribly wrong. He turned blue. He was rushed to the Neonatal Intensive Care Unit where it was determined that he was born with a condition called transposition of the great vessels, which meant that the two major vessels of the heart were reversed, or backward. The baby would die without immediate open-heart surgery to correct the problem. He was taken to another hospital with a pediatric heart specialist and underwent an open-heart procedure. Thankfully, the procedure was a success and this dear little boy survived.

I paused and looked over at Margaret, who was listening intently. I sighed. "You know, Margaret, by this time, I was convinced that God had some kind of purpose for showing me these things in my dreams. I just for the life of me could not figure out what this purpose was. It both frightened and amazed me. I knew I could not have called my friend and told her what I had dreamed. It would have scared her to death, and she probably would have thought that I had lost my mind. But I also was getting the clear impression that *this dreaming was not to be ignored.*"

Margaret stood and walked slowly around the table to stand behind me. She placed both of her hands gently on my shoulders. In a hushed voice, she said, "You were correct, Jennifer, in your impression that you were not to ignore these special dreams.

"I want you to do something now. Close your eyes and picture this in your mind: As a child, dreaming was like resting up against a heavy wooden door with huge rusted iron hinges. Feel it. The door is solid, immoveable, secure. Just like your childhood dreams, it is just there. It may lead somewhere, but you are not particularly interested in where. You are only interested in waking up after a pleasant rest.

"Then, as a young woman, your dreams change. They take on meaning. They come true. They cause you angst. You know there is a purpose, but you don't know what it is. You are curious and are now pressing your hands against the door. Suddenly you hear the sound of huge tumblers falling into place as a great lock becomes unlatched. The rusted hinges creak mightily, and the door cracks open barely an inch with a tremendous shudder. You peek inside, trying to get a glimpse of what is beyond…there is a light approaching…you press harder…

"Now, Jennifer!" Margaret commanded. "Throw open this door! What do you think God was telling you by sending you these dreams?"

Rooted to my chair, I thought for a minute and answered,

"Pay attention, my beloved, and listen to me. I have much to teach you."

"*Whoosh!*" exclaimed Margaret, flinging her arms wide. "The door of innocence flies wide open, and the Light of his truth comes flooding out upon you!"

Relief and joy swept through me as if a mighty wind had just blown through that door. Margaret confirmed what I already knew to be true in my heart. *God unlocked my innocence in order to reach me.* He did not send me these dreams as a whim or to confuse me. He has something important to say, and he uses my dreams to speak to me. *These initial dreams were meant to make me sit up and pay attention because more was coming my way.*

"For reasons known only to him, Jennifer, our Holy Father chose this kind of dreaming to communicate with you. Dreaming is and always has been a very serious and important form of communication between God and his children. The Bible is full of people whom he spoke to in their dreams. Jacob, Joseph, Daniel, Ezekiel, Job, Joseph— father of Jesus—and John, just to name a few. When you are at rest, your mind is free of the clutter of your daily life. The Holy Spirit is able to reach through to your very soul to whisper God's Word to you, and if you are patient, he will reveal its meaning for you. You are now dreaming with the power of the Holy Spirit, and he is revealing important truths. And with this gift comes an equally important responsibility on your part. *To listen, to understand, and when directed, to obey.*

"Dear child, God has given you the gift of 'eyes that see' (Proverbs 20:12 ESV). Your dreams now move between the earthly and spiritual realms. But before we delve into your sacred dreams, there is something else you need to share. God has graced you with another gift of the Spirit, has he not?"

"Oh, yes!" I whispered. "That still small voice. It is the most powerful voice in the universe!"

"Ah yes, my child." Margaret nodded meaningfully. "He has also given you 'ears that hear'" (Proverbs 20:12 ESV).

Eye of the Storm

And he said, "Go out and stand on the mount before the Lord." And behold, the Lord passed by, and a great and strong wind tore the mountains and broke in pieces the rocks before the Lord, but the Lord was not in the wind. And after the wind an earthquake, but the Lord was not in the earthquake. And after the earthquake a fire, but the Lord was not in the fire. And after the fire the sound of a low whisper. And when Elijah heard it, he wrapped his face in his cloak and went out and stood at the entrance of the cave.

1 Kings 19:11–13 (ESV)

A strong wind suddenly began to blow through the backyard and tugged at the large umbrella over our table. Margaret turned and looked toward the northwest, and I heard her say softly, "Here it comes!" Curious, my eyes followed the direction she was looking and saw a sky filled with angry black clouds. A summer cloudburst was fast approaching. A loud rumble of thunder filled the air; and with that, Cody, Hannah, and Isabel raced in from the back of the yard at something approaching warp speed.

Laughing, Margaret shouted above the wind and thunder, "We had better take cover on the porch, Jenn! You get the dogs and I'll put down the umbrella!"

I corralled the dogs, and we hurried to the porch, meeting up with Margaret just before the deluge let loose. The covered porch is deep and wide, providing ample shelter from the rain and wind, so we sat down in a couple of rocking chairs to watch and wait it out. Cody frantically pawed his way into our angel friend's lap, and the two smaller dogs jumped up into mine and snuggled in close. Neither of us had any lap left over!

Margaret giggled. "Well, isn't this cozy!"

For nearly half an hour, we sat rocking quietly while the storm blew, boomed, and poured out its fury. Finally spent, the clouds broke apart, and the warm sun reemerged, creating a landscape that glistened with raindrops.

"Storms have always intrigued me." Margaret sighed. "They can be so powerful, and yet they always pass. Many storms leave destruction in their wake, but that mercifully passes too and is replaced by healing, strength, and beauty nurtured by the storm's elements. Very similar to the storms we experience in life. Don't you agree, Jenn?"

"Y-yeah," I answered hesitantly, unsure of where my friend was going with this point. I began to have an inkling...

Margaret turned in her chair to face me directly, her blue eyes looking into mine. "There is a part of your story we have not yet discussed, Jenn, and it is time. I want you to tell me about the period of your life shortly after you dreamed of the child with the heart condition. You were in your late twenties."

My stomach dropped, and I instinctively clutched the two little dogs in my lap and held them closer to me. "Yes, ma'am, I know what you are referring to." I sighed sadly. "I was kind of hoping to skip over that part."

"This is one of the reasons our Father sent me to help you with this project, my sweet girl," said Margaret gently. "This period of your life is an important part of who you are, and he wants you to include it in your story."

I felt completely humbled and so very much loved at that moment.

I took a deep breath and exhaled. "Okay. Here goes. It was during the late 1980s, and during this period of spiritual awakening, another part of my life was being devastatingly slammed shut. My one and *only* plan for my life was to be a wife and mother. Period. I wanted to be just like my own mother, who is wonderful, caring, and nurturing. For years my husband and I tried to have children with no results and never a definitive diagnosis. I saw infertility specialists, tried various artificial insemination procedures, and despised every second of it. Something that should have been so natural and loving had become clinical and stressful, physically as well as financially. We did not have the money to try the horrendously expensive in vitro fertilization procedure. My friends were all having children and were busy raising their families. I felt so incredibly sad and left out. I stopped seeing many of my friends with children and could not bring myself to attend any of the baby showers that I was invited to. In my attempt to mitigate my pain, separating myself from my friends only served to bring on a whole new wave of anguish.

"In addition, while all this was going on, I was completely unaware that I was suffering from a thyroid imbalance caused by another tumor, which was benign and was later successfully removed. These factors combined to play havoc with my emotions, my health, and my marriage. There were no support groups for this kind of thing back then—no one wanted to talk about infertility. My life spun out of control, and I made hurtful choices. My marriage ended, thankfully not bitterly, and both of us moved on with our lives. I was so ashamed and devastated. I was not at all prepared to have my dreams so thoroughly swept away from me, and guess what? *I became very angry with God.* No God could love me and let this happen to me. I prayed and prayed and *prayed* for God to fix things so I could have children, but my prayers were met with absolute silence. So I quit talking to him."

Margaret reached over and placed her hand on my arm. Her eyes expressed a deep empathy, and I knew then that she had been a witness to all that had happened.

"You went through a terrible storm, Jennifer. I watched what it was like for you, and I grieved along with you. You were lost in the thunder and the wind and the rain, and you could not find God."

"That is a really good description, Margaret. I can give you a little mental picture of what it felt like to me. When I sat in the bathtub as a little girl, I used to be fascinated by pulling the drain plug and watching a mini tornado form as the water was sucked down the drain.

"Well, I felt like I had been sucked up by that tornado and thoroughly ripped and torn from all that I knew and watched as my dreams swirled down the drain. And like being in the vacuum of a tornado, I felt like I couldn't breathe for a very long time.

"But finally, like you said, the storm passed. I began to try to live my life again, but I still felt terribly lost and sad. And I still wasn't talking to God.

"And that is when the most incredible thing happened, Margaret. When I quit talking to him, *he began talking to me!*

"The first time he did so is the first and only time, so far, that I have heard his voice aloud while awake. I was lying in bed, alone, devastated and trying hard to catch the sleep that had been eluding me. My thoughts spun in my head so fast that I could barely keep up. *'What am I going to do now? Why did this happen to me? How can I go through life without children and grandchildren? Who will ever want me for a wife?'* And that is when I heard, out of the darkness, as if someone was standing right next to my bed, *'Jennifer!'* The voice was loud and startled me into complete silence. All those thoughts instantly evaporated, and I was left with the feeling that God was right there in the room, and he was telling me to just *stop, breathe, trust*. And I did just that, because quite frankly, I didn't know what else to do.

"Now that he had my attention again, he began to talk to me in my dreams. I dreamt about my friends, sister, cousins, women who were close to me. In these dreams, a voice would announce that the person I was dreaming about was pregnant. And they were! I was given this knowledge well before their pregnancies were made public. I had never experienced this kind of 'announcing' in a dream before. And I was completely astounded. I mean, here I was, miserable about being childless, and God was giving me dreams about pregnancies! At first, I thought it was some kind of cruel cosmic joke, but then I began to realize that God was just not going to let me turn him off. He was letting me know that even in the midst of my pain, he was still there and he had something to say to me. He had given me a gift, and he was going to make sure I learned how to use it. This voice, this announcing, was something that I could not ignore. I had not forgiven God yet, but I was listening again."

"Our Father is most amazing in his persistence, isn't he, dear one?" Margaret smiled wistfully. "And there was a powerful lesson in the midst of all of this. Can you tell me what you think he hoped you would learn during this painful and difficult time in your life?"

I closed my eyes, took a deep breath, and concentrated on the stillness of my heart, which is where I can always find God. And there, I found my answer:

"Most cherished of my heart, I am in the quiet eye of every storm you will go through. When you are caught up in one of life's storms, run to me, dear one, not away from me."

"Oh, Jenn, that is such a precious truth to carry with you during your life here on earth. And you need to know that it is okay to be angry with God. He is *God*. He can take it! He would much rather you come to him in your anger and despair rather than turn away from him. And his quiet voice, the voice that breathed the entire creation into being, will always guide you right back into his arms. I am so glad that you began to listen to him again!"

A giant lump had formed in my throat, and I wasn't able to speak. As tears welled in my eyes and threatened to spill over, I simply nodded my head in agreement.

Margaret reached over and patted my arm. "Now, child, I need to leave you for a little while. I would like to meet you back here this evening after dark, for there is something special we are going to explore together."

With a mysterious twinkle in her eyes, Margaret gently ushered Cody from her lap and headed out into the glistening wet grass. As she walked into the butterfly garden, her yellow gown shimmered and merged with the yellow lantana flowers, and then she was gone.

I sighed deeply and wiped my eyes. Honestly, I felt a little like Dorothy in the *Wizard of Oz* as she witnessed the beautiful Glinda arrive and depart in a giant bubble. "My goodness, people come and go around here so quickly!"

Savior

In the beginning the Word already existed. The Word was with God, and the Word was God. He existed in the beginning with God. God created everything through him, and nothing was created except through him. The Word gave life to everything that was created, and his life brought light to everyone. The light shines in the darkness, and the darkness can never extinguish it.

John 1:1–5 (NLT)

The shadows of the evening grew into dark. I stepped off the patio and looked in the direction of the garden where I last saw Margaret. *Any minute now,* I thought. *I wonder what Margaret has planned for tonight?* She has ever so gently guided me into discovering new and precious truths in each one of our conversations. This morning's conversation had included a topic that had always been acutely painful for me, yet at its conclusion, I was left with a feeling of being profoundly loved.

The night was warm and peaceful. All the busyness and noise of the day had been put to rest. I listened to the faint rustle of the breeze and the soft music of my wind chimes. Then next to the statue of St. Francis in my Assisi Garden, a faint shimmer of light appeared. It grew steadily brighter, and I again saw the faint outline of wings—my angel was back! Margaret stepped from the garden and came to stand by my side. She smelled faintly of white roses.

"Did you enjoy your day, Jenn?" she asked.

"Yes, I did," I replied. "I did a lot of reflecting on what we talked about and how God's voice called me back to him."

She smiled and I noticed that mysterious twinkle again. "We are going to continue that conversation, and I am so excited because tonight is all about the wonder of his love!" She motioned over to our chairs by the fire pit. "Let's go sit."

We settled into our two chairs looking out into the backyard and sat for a few moments in silence, letting the quiet of the night seep into our hearts. The scent of gardenias was heavy in the air, and little tree frogs began to sing, creating a rhythmic chorus in the darkness.

After a while, Margaret spoke. "Look at all those stars!" She sighed, leaning her head back against the chair and lifting her face to the heavens. "So many beautiful points of light." She turned her head and looked at me, and with a soft voice, she said, "You had a personal encounter with the Original Source of that Light, did you not?"

"Yes." I breathed, looking up at the star-filled sky. "I sure did. I met him in the darkest place I have ever been."

"Tell me," Margaret prodded gently.

My heart quickened as I began to tell Margaret the story of a night and a meeting arranged by the Almighty himself.

"The agony of the years of my infertility and then a failed marriage really took its toll on me. I felt so far away from God and so far away from myself. I had no idea how to get back to that happy, confident young woman that I had been so long ago. I began to see a therapist, who did help me to put things in perspective a bit, but I was still so incredibly *sad*. Then, one night, soon after hearing God speak my name by my bedside, I went to bed and dreamed a dream that changed my life."

As my dream begins, I am walking in a cold, very dark desert. There are no stars, and I am afraid. I don't know what I am afraid of, but it has something to do with being out after dark. For some reason, it is very important to be home after the sun has set or I will be in danger. I walk quickly toward my house in the desert. It is a clay dwelling with open-air arched windows. The dwelling reminds me of something you might see in old Jerusalem. As I walk on the cold sand, my fear rises to an almost panicked level. I have to get to my house soon, but my house is dark, and I am also afraid of what the darkness inside the house might hold for me. As I finally approach my house, I am amazed to see a hand placing a brightly lit candle in the window. No one is supposed to be there! I feel instant relief at that little point

of light—it is the only light I can see for miles around. I enter my home. It has a dirt floor and there is no furniture. I look across the room to where the window is, and what I see astonishes me. There, standing in a shimmering gold light that encompasses his whole being, is Jesus! I fall to my knees before him in absolute wonder. His hand is still on the candle holder in the window as if he is still holding it to light my way. I cannot see the details of his face clearly because of the incredible, shimmering gold light, but I instantly know him. He smiles and his voice says to me, "I will always be here for you, Jennifer." With that, he begins to shimmer even more and starts to fade. The gold shimmers are dispersing in an ever-widening pattern until they engulf the whole room, swirling around me. The very air I breathe is full of him, effervescent. As I breathe in, it feels as if I have been dropped into a very bubbly glass of champagne and am breathing in the liquid bubbles. Then the room becomes quiet. He is gone. But I am no longer afraid. When I awaken from my dream, I feel, for the first time in a very long time, that things are going to be okay. And even better, I also know that I have just met my Savior, the Light of the World.

My beautiful angel and I sat gazing at the stars in silence after I finished my story. Even after all these years, the memory of my meeting with Jesus is still so powerful that it can bring me to my knees.

Margaret's voice gently interrupted my thoughts. "Jenn, have you ever thought about why your dream took place in a desert?"

I thought for a minute. "I guess I always assumed it was because I felt so lonely and left out, just as the desert seems a very lonely place," I answered.

Margaret nodded thoughtfully. Then she said quietly, "The desert is also a very barren place, Jenn. Barren and seemingly lifeless. But when the rains come and the desert is soaked in water, it blooms! Does this resonate with you?"

I winced at her use of the word *barren*. "Oh, Margaret, that word still distresses me. But yes, it does resonate with me. I struggled so much with being childless and hated the word *barren* every time I encountered it. My life seemed empty, without purpose."

"I know, dear child, and what you need to realize is that *you were that desert.* You felt barren and lifeless, until you met Jesus in your dream. Then a miracle happened. You met the source of Light and Living Water, you soaked in his very essence, and you bloomed!"

As I let her words sink in, a memory from my childhood sprang forth. I had actually seen the Arizona desert in bloom after a rainy spring. The cactus flowers were so beautiful! With a happy realization, I knew Margaret was right.

"I guess I did bloom, Margaret! After that dream, things really began to change for me. I regained the confidence I once had, and began picking up the pieces of my life. I had a wonderfully supportive family, a good job, got back in touch with friends, and within a few years married my Guy, who has been my husband for nearly twenty years. And I even got a chance to be a mom by helping to raise his son. Being a stepmom isn't the same as being a mother, but it was the best I was going to get, so I gave my all to a special little boy named Jason who is now a grown-up, independent young man.

"To this very day, Margaret, I am so very touched and humbled to know that in my darkness, my Lord reached out to me and found me. He knew how very much I needed him, even when I didn't. He really does not give up on you."

"No, he does not," agreed Margaret. "I wish more people realized that. Many feel that they are unworthy of God's love. It may be because they have made poor decisions, have made a mess of their lives, or perhaps some even feel that God does not even know they exist. But what people need to understand is that they *are* worthy *because they are his children*. God put each and every person here on this earth and cares deeply for them. All one has to do is to seek him. He will find you and meet you where you are.

"Your dream reminds me of a biblical parallel, Jenn. Do you remember the story in Exodus of the Israelites on the last night of their captivity in Egypt? On that night, God sent the final and most deadly plague against the pharaoh and the Egyptians in order to demonstrate his power as the one true God and to convince the pharaoh to let the Israelites leave the country. The Israelites were instructed to place the blood of a lamb on the doorposts of their homes and to stay inside. That night was dark and terrifying, and they were very afraid. At midnight, the harbinger of death began to creep through the neighborhoods. And then something wonderful happened. It was as if the blood smeared on the doorposts suddenly blazed and pierced the darkness like the brightest of stars, repulsing the evil plague so that it passed over their homes, and the Israelites were spared the deaths of their firstborn. God was the Deliverer of his people. And our beloved Jesus is the New Testament Lamb, who shed his blood for all of humanity that they may be saved from the darkness forever."

"The story of the Exodus is one of my favorites," I replied with a wistful smile. "And I do see the parallel. Jesus, the Lamb of God, certainly did deliver me when he found me in the terrifying night of my dream and led me home with his Light. The Light repelled the fear, the darkness and the oppression I had been feeling for so long.

"And, Margaret, you don't even have to ask me about the message my Lord had for me during this dream and this sad time in my life because my heart knew the answer the instant I met him:

"I am always here for you, my child. No darkness is too dark, no circumstance is too dire for me to walk into with my Light and free you."

"From this point on, I truly gave myself over to God, paying attention to what he said to me in my dreams or through his quiet voice. And speaking of his quiet voice, a new gift was emerging. I began to hear his voice while I was awake. Not out loud, but what I call an 'inside voice.' It is a voice that speaks inside me, clearly and concisely—only a few words at a time, much like a brief statement or command."

"I know that voice well, dear child," said Margaret softly.

We sat contentedly for a few moments, listening to the growing multitude of chirping voices provided by the frogs and crickets. Then my dear angel stood and stretched, and I knew that our evening had drawn to a close.

"This night has been so special, Jenn! I have loved sitting here under the stars with you and hearing about your encounter with Jesus. The starry night sky is a wonderful reminder to humanity of the Light that pierces the darkness. When you think about it, the universe is an unending symbol of hope!

"I want to stop here and let this experience sink deeply into my heart. And you need to get some rest now, Jenn. Sleep sweetly tonight, and I will see you in the morning. Tomorrow, let's speak more about the Almighty's voice.

"Goodnight, dear one!"

"Good night, Margaret," I replied, stifling a yawn.

I leaned back in my chair and watched as she walked back into the shadows and disappeared. Then I turned my eyes once more to the heavens and whispered "good night" to my Savior—my beautiful, shimmering Light.

Whispered Blessings

And the Lord called Samuel again the third time. And he arose and went to Eli and said,

"Here I am, for you called me." Then Eli perceived that the Lord was calling the young man. Therefore Eli said to Samuel, "Go, lie down, and if he calls you, you shall say,

'Speak, Lord, for your servant hears.'" So Samuel went and lay down in his place.

And the Lord came and stood, calling as at other times, "Samuel! Samuel!" And Samuel said, "Speak, for your servant hears."

1 Samuel 3:8–10 (ESV)

The next morning dawned as only one in southeast Texas could—sunny, hot, and steamy. In anticipation of Margaret's arrival, I carried two cups of coffee out onto the patio and set them on the garden table. I then turned my attention to the Frisbee that was most insistently bumping into the backs of my legs. Cody stood there, determined that we get a few throws in before Margaret arrived. I knew it was no use ignoring him because he can be mighty persistent. I marvel at how he can communicate very effectively without audible words! After several throws and long runs through the deep backyard, Cody happily jumped into the pool to cool off. I settled comfortably at the table and closed my eyes, listening to the sounds of the world coming awake. Already, the cicadas were buzzing, calling to each other across the neighboring yards, a distinctive sign that we were deep into summer.

"This is the day that the Lord has made, let us rejoice and be glad in it!" I jumped in my chair, eyes flying open. There was my beautiful angel, laughing and standing behind me. She was radiant. Today her silver blue gown had swirls of pink in it, which matched the slight pink flush of her cheeks. The diamond-like material shimmered in the sun...lovely.

"Good morning, Margaret!"

"And a good morning to you, sweet girl," she replied. "Our Father sends you his dearest love and is so pleased with your progress so far."

More goose bumps. To receive such a personal message from my Lord filled me with awe.

Margaret gracefully swept into the chair next to me and settled herself in. She gave a little squeak of delight as she spied the coffee that I had set on the table for her and indulged in a long, slightly noisy, delicious sip. I tried hard to suppress a giggle. This angel and her coffee cracked me up!

"Last night before I left, Jenn, you mentioned your newly emerging gift of hearing God's voice. I can't wait to hear more about it. Tell me, tell me!" She gleefully rubbed her hands together, her blue eyes twinkling merrily.

"Well, it's kind of hard to describe, but here goes," I replied, giggling at her enthusiasm. "As I mentioned last night, when I hear Gods' voice, it is an inside, internal voice. A whisper. I do not hear him speaking out loud like you and I are doing right now. And he uses very few words, more like a command. The way I recognize the difference between his voice and my own thoughts is that his voice comes when I least expect it, when my mind is occupied by something else. It interrupts. It is clear, concise, and cuts to my very core, pushing aside all other thoughts. Also, his command will often repeat, most likely because the first time I unfortunately have either questioned or ignored it. In this case, his voice will persist until I finally listen and obey.

"I believe a lot of people have this gift, Margaret, yet they do not recognize it as God's voice. It can be in the form of an urge to call someone, to check on a friend, to pray for someone, a sense of danger nearby, all the little quiet nudges that many identify as intuition. I have found that the best way to recognize an 'intuition' as God's voice is if it is a command to do something that will bless you or someone else. Because God is always looking out for the best interests of his children, his voice will never lead you astray.

"A friend once shared a story with me about how she was awakened in the middle of the night by a strong urging to pray for her son, who was many miles away in a big city. Worried, she tried to reach him by phone but was unsuccessful, so she did as the urging instructed. She prayed and prayed. The next morning she learned that her son had been the victim of a mugging but, thankfully, was all right.

"In another example, a woman heard God's quiet voice tell her to purchase multiple copies of Rick Warren's book *The Purpose Driven Life*. Not only did God tell her to purchase the books, he told her *where* to purchase these books, and in the subsequent details, this proved without question that the message came from the Lord himself. She was obedient even though the reason behind the purchase was not clear to her. In time, she understood that God would direct these books to people whose lives would be significantly impacted by reading them. The experience left her feeling overwhelmingly humbled and blessed. I love hearing the stories of others who *do* recognize his voice and are obedient to it!"

Margaret clasped her hands to her heart. "Oh, Jenn, I wish you knew just how *much* that pleases our Father!"

"So now, tell me one of *your* stories about hearing his voice," coached my angel.

"I have several that are particularly meaningful," I replied.

"The first happened several years ago. I had my yearly mammogram and was called back for an ultrasound. During the ultrasound, the radiologist came into the room and asked me if I knew about a mass in my right breast. I replied that yes, I had had it for twenty years or so. It was a suspected fibroid tumor, and no one had ever seemed too concerned about it. He then suggested that it should be biopsied. Grudgingly, I agreed, but my normally active imagination went into overdrive, and I was scared to death. I underwent the procedure and began the five- to seven-day wait for the results. I was a mess. I could not concentrate on anything. I eventually decided to try to go about my normal routine as much as possible to keep my mind occupied. One morning, while applying my makeup, two words suddenly interrupted and said quite clearly in my heart, "*Blessed Assurance.*" I was surprised, to say the least, but it did give me a little bit of comfort. As the day progressed, every time I started to worry again, those same two words would interrupt. Several days later and still no pathology report, I headed to the Methodist Hospital in Houston, where I volunteered as a lay minister. In short, a lay minister is a non-clergy person trained by the spiritual care (chaplain) department to visit with patients—to listen to them and to pray with them.

"I was assigned to a medical floor and the transplant unit. My mentor chaplain was a wonderful woman named Michelle. I stopped in to see Michelle before I went up to the transplant unit to begin my visits. She asked me how I was doing, and I broke down in tears and told her what was going on. When I told her that I kept hearing two words in my heart, she asked me what they were. When I told her *Blessed Assurance*, her reaction was amazing! She looked at me stunned and said, 'Jennifer, that is my favorite hymn!' *Hymn?* I had no idea. She jumped up and pulled a hymnal from her bookshelf and turned it to, sure enough, the hymn *Blessed Assurance.* We read the hymn together and then we prayed together. The words of the hymn were such comfort. What a healing moment that was! How wonderful that my Father in heaven would use the words from a hymn to speak to me, when he knows that music is so dear to my heart. I just knew that things would be okay, and later that day, I learned that my biopsy results were benign."

Margaret sighed. "It is no wonder to me that he used the words of a hymn to speak to you. *He created your inmost being. He knit you together in your mother's womb.* He knows your heart and loves you so very much, precious one!"

My heart swelled with love as I heard her words.

"God spoke to me again through music in my next story. Several years ago, Guy and I moved away from our friends and beloved church home in League City and relocated to this area north of Houston. It was a good move for us, but I missed my friends and church family terribly and did not know a single person up here. I began a search for a new church while Guy was traveling overseas. I visited several churches the size of our former church (approximately eight hundred members) but did not find anything to 'fit' me and my spiritual and worship needs. When Guy returned home, he suggested that we try a large United Methodist Church near our home. I had been there once for a week as a delegate to Texas Annual Conference several years before, and I knew how big this church was (approximately ten thousand members). It has a large sanctuary and also a more intimate, lovely chapel.

"I was intimidated by the size of this church and confided to my husband that I was afraid I would not be able to find my way among so many people. How would I ever get to know anyone in a church this size? So Guy suggested that we start small and attend a 9:30 a.m. chapel service.

"Sunday morning arrived, and while I was busy getting dressed, a couple of words suddenly planted themselves into my heart and mind: '*How Beautiful.*' *Why, thank you, Father!* I thought playfully, thinking he had just paid me a compliment."

Another very un-angel-like snort erupted from the chair next to me. I glanced over to see Margaret rolling her eyes.

"I know, I know, just my vanity rearing its ugly head!" I said quickly, before she could. "I figured out pretty quickly that those words meant something else because they kept repeating over the next half an hour or so as we continued to get ready to go to church. When we arrived at the church, the service was about to start, so we quickly found some seats. Not too far into the service, a musician began to play a flute solo. It was such a lovely melody, and I glanced down at my bulletin to see what the song was titled. Imagine my astonishment to see printed in the bulletin the words '*How Beautiful.*' I leaned over and whispered to Guy, 'You know those words I told you were running through my head this morning while I was getting ready? It is the name of this song. . . look! Isn't that *weird?*' Guy leaned over to me with a grin and whispered, '*No*, Jenn, *you're* weird!' My sweet husband is used to these revelations of mine, bless his heart!

"And the morning just kept getting more amazing. The scripture reading from Mark 5:25–34 was the story of the hemorrhaging woman in a crowd of people surrounding Jesus who reached out in faith to touch Jesus's cloak. Jesus felt the power leave him and asked, 'Who touched me?' When the woman acknowledged her action, Jesus told her that 'your faith has made you well.' That has always been one of my very favorite scriptures. Then during his sermon, the pastor told a story about his grandmother who experienced visions, and he described an encounter she had with her son that had died. I remember him saying something to the effect that he didn't know how we all felt about people having visions, but his grandmother believed that what she experienced was real. It was as if he was speaking to me directly, and I felt like Jesus was sitting right next to me, saying, 'See, Jennifer, this church is where you need to be. I have given you several signs today that you can be comfortable and find purpose here.' Well, he didn't have to whack *me* over the head with a two-by-four anymore. I got his message loud and clear and felt humbled and at peace that this would be my new church home and that my Lord had selected it for me. And I will tell you, Margaret, that being a member of this church has been an overwhelming blessing to me and has helped me to grow as a Christian. I joined the choir and met many wonderful new friends and have been able to get back to teaching Bible study, which has been a passion of mine for many years."

"Oh, my dear Jennifer, God has a specific plan for your life, and you are seeing it unfold before your very eyes. It is so important to realize that you are where he wants you to be at this moment in time. And I am so thankful you have learned to listen to what he says to you," said Margaret purposefully. She leaned back in her chair and lifted her face to the sun. "In fact, the very angels of heaven rejoice when God's people learn to listen and obey his voice, because sometimes his command will have an eternal significance in the life of one of his beloved children."

Margaret then turned to me, and her face had taken on a serious look. "You have a story that is a poignant illustration of how important it is to listen and obey. Do you know which experience I am referring to?"

"I do, Margaret. It was one of the most humbling experiences of my life."

The memory of this encounter still tugs at my heart.

"The experience you are referring to took place when, again, I was at the Methodist Hospital doing my lay ministry visits. Before beginning my visits on the floors to which I was assigned, I routinely prayed a short prayer, asking God to empty me so that I could fully serve him and the patients I visited. My inspiration for this was from Philippians 2:7 when Christ 'emptied himself, by taking the form of a servant' (ESV). For, without first laying all of my own needs, concerns, to-do lists, etc., at his feet, I would not be able to give all of myself to the patients and their needs, whether it was prayer, someone to talk to, or to just sit quietly and listen. My prayer always ended with a request that God would guide me to those that needed his comfort that day. I have many examples of the wonderful ways he answered that prayer, every single time I served as a lay minister, steering me to particular patient rooms, giving me appropriate words of prayer—the list is long. But this one particular experience will stay with me forever in its example of how he used me to help minister to one of his beloved children.

"I had completed my rounds on the medical floor, which had taken longer than usual due to a full census and many patient visits, and I arrived on the transplant unit already emotionally weary. This was a very special floor. The patients I visited with could be in one of three different stages: awaiting a transplant, immediate post transplant, or experiencing problems with or rejection of their transplant. I was issued a daily census listing the patient names and room numbers and began my journey around the huge U-shaped floor. I had a couple of visits, but many patients were either sleeping or absent from their rooms so I began to feel that my day would soon be over. I headed down the backstretch of the U-shape and paused at the room of a patient whose name I did not recognize. The door was slightly ajar, and when I looked in, there were several physicians in the room. Protocol indicated that I skip a room when a physician is in attendance, so I went on my way and ended up at the end of the floor. Whew! My day was done, and I was tired. I headed to the elevators and pressed the Down button. Suddenly, a very strong inside voice commanded (and I mean *commanded*) '*Go back to that room!*'

"*Oh, come on!* I thought, rolling my eyes. *Not now. I am really tired and that room was full of doctors.* I pressed the Down button again. Once more the voice commanded, '*Turn around and go back to that room!*' Okay, that time the voice sounded a little mad, so I let out an exasperated sigh, whirled around, and walked back to the patient's room that had been full of doctors. Well, to my surprise, the room was now empty except for the patient.

"I knocked softly on the open door and walked in, finding the patient sitting in a chair next to his bed. When I looked at him, I recognized him as a man I had visited with in prior weeks. 'Well, hello!' I said. 'How are you doing today?'

"'Oh!' he exclaimed. 'I am so glad you came back to see me! I saw you walk by when all the doctors were here a few minutes ago, and I was afraid you might not come back!'

"Now, this is when I started to realize God was up to something special. I remembered that this man was one of those on a waiting list for a heart transplant. He had some sort of artificial implant that was keeping his heart going and knew that each day was a race against time. Apparently, the news the doctors had just given him was not very encouraging. We talked a long time about his feelings, and he asked me to pray with him before I left. He was such a dear man, and together, we participated in a very personal time of prayer with our Lord. When we were through, he held my hands and thanked me and asked me to come back and see him when I returned the next week.

"The next week when I returned to the transplant floor, I did not see this man's name on the census, so I inquired about him. I was told very gently by the nurse that he had had a major stroke the morning after I had visited with him last week and went into a coma. After several days, he died, never regaining consciousness. My heart was broken for that sweet little man. But I was overwhelmed by what the Lord had done for his beloved child. He made sure that this man had been ministered to and had the opportunity to go to his Lord in prayer before he died. And he used me to help make that possible. I was completely and utterly humbled, as well as privately ashamed at my initial reaction to my Lord's command to go back to that room. I am *so* very glad that I decided to listen and obey his voice that day!"

Margaret looked over at me, and I saw that her face was streaming with tears. She smiled a little crookedly and made a sign with her hand as if to say "keep going" since she was too emotional to speak at the moment.

So I continued with a thought that had been on my mind for a while.

"I know that there have been many times in my life when I have either completely missed or, even worse, just ignored God's voice. So often I have felt an urge to act, to give someone an unexpected hug, or heard a whisper to call someone, yet just passed it off as my imagination. I wonder how many opportunities to minister to someone I have missed by doing so. It makes my heart hurt to think about it because it has become so clear to me how much our Creator cares for each and every one of us. Knowing that he has continued talking to us through the ages, yet so many times he is not heard is a serious concern to me. I can only imagine what this world would be like if more people listened for his voice and acted upon it. *Thy will be done, on Earth as it is in Heaven.*"

Margaret was still overcome with tears, and by now I knew that she would want me to answer a question. 'What was the lesson that God had for me as I began to listen to and obey his voice?'

I reached over, took her hand in mine, and gave her my answer:

"*Listen to me, beloved child, and do as I ask. You do not have to understand why. Each and every time, when my voice is heard and obeyed, someone is blessed.*"

Margaret

Lord Hear My Prayer

The Language of God

Garden Party

3-D Vision

In the last days, God says, I will pour out my Spirit on all people. Your sons and daughters will prophesy, your young men will see visions, your old men will dream dreams. Even on my servants, both men and women, I will pour out my Spirit in those days and they will prophesy. I will show wonders in the heaven above and signs on the earth below, blood and fire and billows of smoke. The sun will be turned to darkness and the moon to blood before the coming of the great and glorious day of the Lord. And everyone who calls on the name of the Lord will be saved.

Acts 2:17–21; Joel 2:28–32 (NIV)

Margaret slowly got up from her chair, brushing away the tears that continued to stream down her cheeks. Clearing her throat, she said, "Forgive my Kleenex moment, Jenn, that was such a moving testimony! You have learned much about how and why our Lord speaks to his children, and its significance has not been lost on you. You must always keep this gift close to your heart and follow his direction. He will faithfully steer your feet along his path for you, and he will always lead you and others to his truth.

"Now, if you will excuse me for a moment, I need to go attend to my rather tear-stained eyes and face!" With that, she walked across the patio to the back door and let herself into the house.

I sat for a moment, wondering if I should go inside and help her. But then I decided that she *was* an angel, after all, and had been looking after me all these years, so she probably did not need any assistance from me. I leaned back in my chair, absorbing the warm sunshine, and watched a couple of bluebirds investigate an empty birdhouse in the yard. I wondered hopefully if they were getting ready to raise a new brood of chicks as they had earlier in the spring.

"Okay! All better now!" exclaimed my angel as she strolled out the back door and onto the patio. "How do I look? Nice?" I turned to look at Margaret and laughed out loud. There she stood, posing dramatically in a model's stance with one hand on her hip, an exaggerated smile showing all of her perfect small white teeth and wearing an enormous pair of black horn-rimmed sunglasses. She looked ridiculous and very funny! I got up and walked over to where she stood.

"What in the world?" I laughed. "*Where* did you get those silly glasses?"

"Don't you recognize them, Jenn? They were on your kitchen counter."

"Oh yeah," I exclaimed as I looked closer. "Those are the 3-D glasses I brought home from the movie

Guy and I saw the other night. Why are you wearing those? There isn't anything unusual you can see with them right now, *is there?*"

Margaret grinned and linked her arm through mine, leading me back to our chairs overlooking the yard. We sat, and she pulled out another pair of glasses from the folds of her gown... she must have found both pairs inside. "Here," she said, "put these on."

I put on my 3-D glasses with a giggle and looked at Margaret. We must really look goofy sitting out here in these enormous black glasses! Margaret giggled too, and then, oh my, a hilarious little snort escaped from her mouth! We both erupted in laughter so hard it made my sides ache. She is just the coolest angel ever!

"Okay, seriously now," said Margaret, trying to put a likewise serious look on her face. Somehow, she actually achieved it while I, on the other hand, sat there still grinning ear-to-ear and looking like a complete dork.

"I wanted us to wear these to illustrate a point. When you went to the movie the other night, you had to wear these glasses to see a dimension that was hidden from your normal vision. Is that not correct?"

"Yes!" I replied. "And it was really cool. Everything looked so realistic and clear. Actually, the characters looked as if they were standing right there in front of me!"

"That's right," said Margaret. "Remember when I told you earlier that you were now dreaming with the power of the Holy Spirit? These dream visions have come to you from another realm that is unseen to human eyes. Just like these amazing glasses, our Father has gifted you with the ability not only to dream these visions, but also to see the truth behind them. I have heard you tell others close to you that these dreams are more vivid, more real, and have a presence that your 'regular' dreams do not have, and you are right, because they are inspired by the Holy Spirit, ordained by God himself. And now, the time has come for you to share the sacred dream visions he has sent to you from the realm of heaven."

More goose bumps. My heart constricted from the depth of emotion this subject triggers within me. It is a gift I have held close to my heart for many years and have shared it with very few people. To share it now made me feel a bit melancholy, as if I were going to share a precious child with the world—one I had lovingly protected and nurtured.

"Margaret," I said softly, "these dreams are so special to me. I want very much to honor my Lord's revelations by my interpretation of them. Sometimes my understanding of the message in a dream is immediate, but often, it takes time, even years, for his message to be made clear. You know me and how often it takes me a while to *get it*," I said with a small laugh.

"Dear child, trust in the gift he gave you," said Margaret with a smile of her own. "I have witnessed firsthand how your heart and spirit are moved when a truth is revealed. But humor me anyway. Tell me what it is like for you when you experience a revelation of God's divine truth."

Thoughtfully, I began to tell her what it is like to experience this spiritual gift of visions. "My very first clue, Margaret, that I have experienced a dream vision is that the realism of the dream is extraordinary and the memory does not fade as normal dreams do. I can recall every detail of these dreams, even after many years, as if I was watching a movie. While dreaming a vision that is of the everyday 'secular' world, when I am permitted to see human events that are to happen or are in the process of happening, I am primarily an observer. When dreaming a vision that is sacred, where a spiritual message is involved, I am an active participant. For me, the key to being able to recognize a dream as a sacred vision is that the content is consistent with Holy Scripture.

"Both types of dream visions are extraordinarily rich in their clarity and realistic experience. There is a presence of an intellect other than my own. It is deep, pervasive and wise. Upon awakening from the dream, I am overcome with the knowledge that I have experienced a message from the Almighty.

"And to be candid, while some of my dream visions are happy and exciting, others are quite frightening and have left me with a persistent dose of worry or anxiety. When I experience a sacred vision, there is no accompanying interpretation. Other than a few very obvious meanings, my understanding of God's message comes only after I awaken, when I contemplate the dream's events and submit to prayer and subsequent study of scripture. *The most significant thing I have learned is that these visions speak to the very character of God.* God is not linear. He is the God of past, present, and future, and my visions reflect that. Images I see may be in present time because that is where I exist, yet his messages incorporate past, present, and future events all at the same time. The Bible, his Living Word, is the same way, which is why study of scripture has lead me to an understanding of my visions.

"I cannot tell you, Margaret, how it feels to be in study, reading a section of scripture I have not read before, and *wham*! Suddenly a dream vision I had in the past will be explained so startlingly clearly and completely that it takes my breath away. Once, I was so surprised that I slammed my Bible shut while reading in the book of Revelation. It was about one of my dreams! I was startled enough that it took me a while to get up the courage to crack open my Bible again and take another look at the text. Although I had formed my own basic interpretation of the dream years before, the passage I read and subsequent other readings of scripture brought it all together, and I finally understood the message God intended for me. It is like experiencing a rose unfolding one petal at a time.

"So I guess what I am trying to say, Margaret, is that the dream interpretations I share from this point forward have come from years of prayer, study of scripture, consultation with trusted biblical scholars, and keeping my heart and mind open to his voice. I am fully aware that the interpretation of biblical text does not have universal agreement and that others may hold different interpretations of the scriptures I refer to. Because the Word of God is a Living Word, I never consider my interpretation to be complete. I put my trust in the Holy Spirit to continue to guide my thoughts and my opinions in order to arrive at the lesson that my Lord has for *me*. And a message that a particular dream may hold for me may differ from a message perceived or understood by someone else. That is what is so awesome about God! *He speaks to us where we are.* He is constantly revealing if we are committed to learning and listening. You could say that it is like putting on these 3-D glasses and seeing something absolutely wondrous revealed!"

"Well said, Jennifer! Our Lord God has opened your eyes to show you hidden wonders of his truth!" said Margaret, clapping her hands delightedly. "Listen to this precious moment in scripture when God opened the eyes of Elisha's servant to reveal an incredible sight."

> When the servant of the man of God got up early the next morning and went outside, there were troops, horses, and chariots everywhere. "Oh, sir, what will we do now?" the young man cried to Elisha. "Don't be afraid!" Elisha told him. "For there are more on our side than on theirs!" Then Elisha prayed, "O Lord, open his eyes and let him see!" The Lord opened the young man's eyes, and when he looked up, he saw that the hillside around Elisha was filled with horses and chariots of fire.
>
> 2 Kings 6:15-17 (NLT)

"Oh, Margaret!" I exclaimed. "That is just what I feel the Lord has said to me:

"I have opened your eyes, precious child, so that you may see the wonders of my kingdom!"

"Well then, my girl, let's delve right into these dreams of yours!" Margaret removed her 3-D glasses, leaned back in her chair, let out a deep sigh of contentment, and closed her eyes, ready to listen.

I decided to keep my 3-D glasses on while I began to speak of dreams.

Pilgrimage

*In days to come the mountain of the Lord's house
shall be established as the highest of the mountains,
and shall be raised above the hills; all the nations
shall stream to it. Many peoples shall come and say,
come, let us go up to the mountain of the Lord, to
the house of the God of Jacob; that he may teach us
his ways and that we may walk in his paths.*

Isaiah 2:2–3 (NRSV)

*I am carrying a small suitcase. I look ahead of me and realize
I am in a very long, winding line of people, all carrying
suitcases like me. We are in a beautiful valley. The line snakes
gently over small rolling green hills and leads to a large
mountain ahead in the distance. I wonder to myself, "Where
in the world am I, and more importantly, where am I going?"
I sense the same vague type of mystery from the people around
me, curiously mixed with a feeling of excited anticipation.
We smile and nod to each other as we slowly walk along.*

Suddenly, a man appears directly in front of me, wearing jeans and a dark brown T-shirt. The curious thing about his T-shirt is that it has on it a line of little white sheep, which wrap in a band all the way around the shirt, right at chest level. The even curious-er thing is that the sheep are moving! As if they, too, are walking in a line! Now, this man is beautiful—absolutely, strikingly beautiful. He has dark hair, a closely trimmed beard and mustache, and eyes that sparkle with such extraordinary radiance and excitement that I can't even tell what color they are. He speaks directly to me, and with a smile that reflects the radiance in his eyes, he exclaims, "Isn't this wonderful? Isn't this exciting?" He then steps aside to give me a view of the mountain ahead of us. People are now streaming up one side of the mountain and down the other, and at the very top of the mountain is Jesus! I guess that this must be an angel speaking with me, and his pure joy and excitement catch like a wildfire in my heart. We are on a journey to see Jesus!

My Interpretation of God's Message

As I awakened, I became aware of a huge smile that was spreading across my face. The joy and anticipation I felt in the dream was still with me. The angel with the beautiful smile and eyes so alive with excitement is as clear in my memory today as he was twenty or more years ago when I had the dream. I have slowly but steadily formed an understanding of this dream throughout the years and experienced a particular moment of clarity while studying the Psalms of Ascent (Ps. 120–134). This is a collection of fifteen psalms, or songs, which were sung by the Israelites as they journeyed to and from Jerusalem three times a year to celebrate Passover and the harvest feasts at the Temple in Jerusalem. This type of journey that the Israelites took every year was called a pilgrimage, and I pictured in my mind large groups of extended families making these pilgrimages together—cooking and camping out by night; riding, walking, and visiting by day—filled with anticipation of arriving in their beloved city and celebrating the harvest feast together in the presence of God. And all the while they sang songs handed down from generation to generation to pass the time and to express the joy of their journey. I realized that I had similar memories of my own family travels—singing songs and playing games to pass the time, each of us full of excitement and anticipation of arriving at our destination and the fun that awaited us.

While studying these Psalms of Ascent, I vacationed with my husband and parents in Old Orchard Beach, Maine. It was my first visit to Maine and it was beautiful. The beach was wide and long, the sun was bright, and we had many cool breezes, a wonderful respite from the suffocating summer heat of Houston. One morning early in the week, I pulled out my Bible after getting myself settled on the beach. I began to read the psalms while other people began filing down to the beach with their chairs and towels and beach bags. It was very quiet—just the sound of the waves of the distant tide. After a while, I began to hear the soft strumming of a guitar accompanied by several voices singing along. I glanced over and saw an ever-growing circle of people sitting in the sand, laughing, talking, and holding their coffee cups, obviously enjoying each others' company. Every once in a while, another person would arrive and was greeted with great joy and big hugs all around. I learned from my parents that this was a large reunion of a French Canadian family. Several of them travel to this spot every year, but this particular gathering would include many that had not seen each other in years, and a big feast was planned later in the week when there would be at least fifty family members in attendance.

This was a musical family, and soon other instruments appeared, more voices joined the singing, and they were singing in French. It was so beautiful to listen to that I had a hard time concentrating on my reading. Then I was struck by a most amazing revelation. Isn't this remarkably similar to what was happening in the Psalms of Ascent, as the Israelites made their pilgrimage to Jerusalem? Families that traveled together, loved one another, and sang together, filled with excitement and anticipation of arriving at their destination, their journey culminating in a great celebration feast...a celebration of love? Even I was included, as I had traveled a great distance from Texas to Maine to spend a week with my beloved parents. Suddenly the centuries had melted away, and I was a member of the peoples of the pilgrimage—God's people. As I thought this very thought, a voice inside me said, "*It is all tied together, Jennifer!*" My breath caught in my throat. I slammed my study book shut, closed my eyes, and prayed, "Praise you, Father! Thank you!" I opened up my book again and wrote those words and the date on the page.

It *is* all tied together, because immediately thoughts came so quickly to me that I barely had time to write them down. My thoughts literally flew back to the dream I had had many years before. In my dream, I was on a journey, a pilgrimage with many others. We were the sheep of the angel's T-shirt, and the angel was watching over us, as a shepherd does. The last line of Psalm 121 says, "The Lord keeps watch over you as you come and go, both now and forever" (NLT). The beautiful angel in my dream was so excited for us that he could barely contain his joy. As he stepped away to let me have a view of what lay ahead, I saw a mountain, with people streaming up and down, and Jesus, in silhouette, was at the very top of the mountain. Isaiah 2:2–3 states, "In days to come the mountain of the Lord's house shall be established as the highest of the mountains, and shall be raised above the hills; all the nations shall stream to it. Many peoples shall come and say, come, let us go up to the mountain of the Lord, to the house of the God of Jacob; that he may teach us his ways and that we may walk in his paths" (NRSV). My understanding of this portion of my dream is that we, as beloved children of God, are all on a journey on this earth. We are on a pilgrimage to meet our Savior, the living source of love, grace, and truth. This journey is unique to each one of us: some of us are seeking and discovering; some of us are already experiencing new life in Christ, and still others are reflecting his love and teaching his ways to others.

I also discovered something particularly revealing regarding the feasts involved in the three Old Testament Hebrew pilgrimages mentioned earlier. Each of these feasts celebrates a harvest during the year. Passover/Feast of Unleavened Bread/Feast of First Fruits is celebrated in early spring. The Feast of Weeks is held in early summer, and the Feast of Tabernacles is held in the fall—the final harvest festival.

The New Testament Christian celebrations of Good Friday, Easter, and Pentecost parallel the harvest feasts of the Old Testament and are held at the same time of year, in spring and early summer. There is, however, one Old Testament feast that has not yet been celebrated in the New Testament times: the Feast of Tabernacles, which is the final harvest. Only when Christ returns will he gather his people to him in the final harvest.

So how does it relate to my dream?

Remember the voice that said "*It is all tied together, Jennifer!*" The pilgrimage traditions begun by God's faithful people in the Old Testament have continued through the centuries to our present day, *and we are part of it!* Standing with many others in an unending line with my suitcase in hand, *I was an active participant in this ancient tradition.* We are living in a time that is parallel to the tradition of the Feast of Weeks or Pentecost—the early summer harvest when the Word of God is spreading throughout the world and believers are coming in greater numbers to Christ each and every day.

The era of the final feast, the Feast of Tabernacles, the final harvest and ingathering of God's people, is on the horizon and may be fast approaching. We must be ready, must live each day with a sense of anticipation, and must take seriously our Lord's command to go out and "make disciples of all nations" (Matthew 28:19 ESV). The snapshot I have in my mind of the long line of people in my dream streaming to the mountain is like looking down on the Earth from God's point of view— watching his beloved children march along the timeline span of the ages, from Old Testament days to the present day and into the future. Marching toward him. And one glorious day, all of us, all nations, will come to the mountain of the Lord, just as Isaiah has foretold. No wonder the angel in my dream was so excited for us! Our journey, our *pilgrimage*, will not end until Jesus himself returns to establish his reign on earth, and we shall enter into his kingdom! Just imagine the joyous feast we will celebrate together! Isn't it wonderful? Isn't it exciting? *It* is *all tied together!*

Margaret turned to face me as I finished speaking. Her eyes sparkled and flashed with excitement just like the beautiful angel's eyes in my dream. So much so that it was as if they were lit from within by a holy fire. The intensity of her gaze held mine, and I was secretly glad that I was still wearing the 3-D glasses.

"I still haven't gotten to the most amazing part, Margaret! I held out the best for last!" I continued as a huge grin spread across my face. "And this is a perfect example of how God continues to reveal precious truths even when I think I have a vision all figured out! Just very recently while reading on a flight from Ohio to Houston, I happened upon a drawing of Christ entitled *Prince of Peace*. It was painted by a young girl named Akiane Kramarik, a child prodigy and visionary. When I beheld this image of Christ, it literally took my breath away. The man looking back at me from the painting was the very 'angel' I saw in my dream, the one full of excitement for us and our journey. *It wasn't an angel, Margaret, it was Jesus!* That knowledge adds a whole new dimension of meaning to this vision, on a very personal level, because now I understand that Jesus is watching, he is guiding, and he is bursting with love and excitement for us as we journey toward him! He is not just waiting for us to reach him. He is with us every step of the way!"

I paused for a moment to think about the T-shirt he was wearing with the sheep on it...*I* was one of those little sheep! More goose bumps!

"You most certainly are on the journey of a lifetime, my dear child!" agreed Margaret enthusiastically. "And isn't it wonderful that we have a Father that loves to surprise us by sending us special little gifts along the way that make our hearts sing with gladness? What a joyful revelation he saved for you about the 'angel' in your dream!

"There was so much in your dream that touched your heart deeply. Can you tell me what message held the most importance for you?"

My heart swelled with the remembered excitement I felt in my dream.

"The past, present, and future are all tied together, dear one, and I watch with joy and excitement your earthly journey toward me."

Trinity

Long ago God spoke to our ancestors in many and various ways by the prophets, but in these last days he has spoken to us by a Son, whom he appointed heir of all things, through whom he also created the worlds. He is the reflection of God's glory and the exact imprint of God's very being, and he sustains all things by his powerful word.

Hebrews 1:1–3 (NRSV)

Still marveling over the revelation that we are lovingly and joyfully shepherded through life by Jesus, I finally removed my 3-D glasses. As I laid them on the table, several sharp barks interrupted my thoughts. Looking over toward the house, I saw all three dogs huddled around the door, scratching and whining to be let inside. *How odd,* I thought, *it is such a nice day outside.* The pups were quite insistent, so I gathered up the 3-D glasses and walked over to let them into the house.

Stepping back out onto the porch, I sensed strangeness in the air. It was still nice out, but there was an oppressive feeling that hadn't been there a few minutes before. *Hmmm, maybe it is some atmospheric thing that dogs can sense and humans cannot.* I walked back over to the garden to join Margaret, and as I sat down in my chair, I was stunned to see that a miraculous change had taken place in my angel friend's appearance. Her entire being was radiating a glow of light that formed a halo all around her. The color of her gown had taken on a decidedly shimmering silver hue, and a huge silver shield now rested at her side against her chair. Light continued to radiate from her eyes, making those merry blues look somewhat fierce in their intensity. My sweet, funny Margaret was now appearing to me as the "guardian" in guardian angel!

She rose from her chair, and I noticed that she was significantly taller. I did not speak because I knew she was gearing up to say something important. I was too overwhelmed by what I was witnessing to say anything coherent anyway.

"Jennifer, in your life's journey with our Lord, you have learned a great deal about listening to him and that his messages may take time to understand. As with the interpretation of your last dream, your understanding evolved over time. This is because the Word of God speaks to us where we are, and he teaches us as we are ready to receive. And now, our Father has deemed you ready for some messages of great importance."

Just as she finished speaking, a strong breeze suddenly picked its way through the tree branches above. I looked up as clouds began to swirl overhead in a darkening sky. The breeze increased until it was no longer a breeze but a steady wind, picking up leaves and sending them skittering around the yard and across the patio. Startled birds took flight and went in search of the protection of a nest or secure tree branch. At first, I thought this might be another approaching summer storm, but when I looked up at the dark clouds racing above our heads, I knew that was not the case. I had never seen anything like this. The air turned chilly, and I saw dark shapes flitting in and out of the swirling mass above. The sense of oppression grew heavy, and I began to feel afraid.

Margaret reached out and took my hand in hers. Immediately, the fear and sense of oppression I was experiencing vanished! And oddly, Margaret and I were completely unaffected by the wind. It was as if we were enclosed in a safe cocoon. *Uh-oh*, I thought, *here comes another one of those serious heavenly angel moments!*

"Jennifer, I want you to stay seated so that you will remain within our protective cover," instructed Margaret. Her voice was now much louder and commanding. *Our* protective cover? I covertly tried to peer around me, wondering if there was something or someone else I was not seeing, but of course, I saw nothing. Margaret continued. "The next two dreams we are going to explore were powerful and a bit frightening, wouldn't you agree?"

"Yes, they were," I answered, my heart beginning to pound.

Margaret leaned down slightly and looked directly at me, her intense blue eyes now reflecting a steel gray hue, penetrated mine. "Jenn, do you know what spiritual warfare is?"

"Um, I think so," I replied cautiously, dreading where this was going. "I believe that it is the constant battle being fought in the spiritual realm by God and his angels against Satan and his minions."

"You are quite correct, Jenn, and that is why you are seeing me in this warrior countenance. Spiritual warfare was active while you were dreaming these next two dreams. God sent me and others much mightier than me to guard you while you dreamed and received his messages. Make no mistake, *the Enemy did not want you to remain in a dream state to receive God's message.* You needed help and we were there. Listen now to the Word of God: 'For he will command his angels concerning you to guard you in all your ways'" (Psalm 91:11 ESV).

Gulp! That was a sobering thought! All I did was sleep and dream while the powers of light and darkness waged a war around me. It was frightening but at the same time strangely comforting (yet I admit that I was at that moment seriously considering purchasing a night light for use in the foreseeable future!).

As if she could read my thoughts, Margaret laughed softly and said, "Don't be concerned, this happens all day long, every day, Jennifer! God is always watching over his children and fiercely defends those who bear his mark on their souls."

She picked up her shield, walked over to where I sat in my chair, stood behind me, and placed her right hand on my shoulder. Her grip was so firm and determined that it kind of hurt. "I will remain right here while you speak of your next two dreams…Let's begin."

The night is ink black as I run down the street to get back to my home. Others are doing the same, knowing full well that we are in great danger. Just as I leap into my house and slam the door closed, a tremendous house-shaking roar fills the air, accompanied by a blinding bright light. Immediately there is a large explosion, and I hear screams of agony outside. I do not dare open my door, because I have no idea when another of the harbingers of death will fall from the sky. It has been happening all night and I am exhausted. I want the morning to come so badly, because I know that with the dawn we will have a respite from the death and destruction until the following dusk, when it will all begin again. Some on the news are saying it is solar flares; others say the stars are falling. All I know is that they are points of light that fall indiscriminately from the sky and slam into the earth. Several more of these things fall throughout the night, and all I can hear are explosions and the agonized screams of people caught outside. I am aware that I am dreaming and try to wake up, but it doesn't work, so I hide in a bathtub for the rest of the night. Finally, it falls quiet as the light of dawn fills the sky.

Breathing easier now that the new day has arrived, I get up and prepare myself to go outside and try to attend to anyone that may need some help. With some surprise, I notice that I am very pregnant. I walk slowly down the road, stepping carefully so as not to trip on the large amount of debris and rubble. I do not see any people, injured or otherwise, so I assume they must have already been helped or have found shelter. It is so very quiet. All I can hear is gravel and broken glass crunching beneath my feet. Suddenly, I realize that I am in labor and am going to give birth right here on the street. I deliver my baby in a hospital laundry cart. It is a little boy! I pull him up into my lap and am amazed at how big he is—he looks to be the size of a two year old. He looks up at me with admiring big blue eyes, and then astonishingly he says, "Hello, Mother!" and smiles at me. We stand, he takes my hand, and we walk back to the house together. It is mind-boggling that this newborn child is so grown-up, can walk, talk, is naked, and he completely takes charge, as if he is the one taking care of me. I literally do not have a word to say, all I can do is smile at him.

The day passes, apparently peacefully, because the next scene I remember is walking down to the shore of a large, peaceful lake with my beautiful boy. He still wears no clothes, and he stands at the silvery water's edge, turning to look at me with his wonderful smile. I begin feeling anxious as I notice that the sun is low in the orange sky behind him. With the setting of the sun, the terror from the skies will return. I call out to my child that it is time for us to go home. He stays where he is at the water's edge and says to me, "Mother, I have to go to my father now." "Your father?" I reply, mystified. I have no idea who this child's father is. "Yes, Mother," he replies, "my father is the sun." He turns away from me and points directly at the setting sun. With that, he begins to wade deeper into the water. "No! No! Child, don't go in the water, you will drown!" I cry out. My beautiful boy turns back to me and smiles. "Don't worry, Mother, I will be just fine. I am going to my father now, but I will always be near if you need me." With that, he wades out into the calm silver water toward the setting sun and disappears. Strangely, his words have a great calming effect on me, and I no longer worry about my child. I turn and leave the lake behind me.

Time passes, and in the next scene, I am being swept through the middle of town in a raging river. I, along with many other people, am fighting to keep my head above water as we are pushed along by the strong current. I can see shops and docks along the riverbank and lots of debris floating in the water with us, as if this is some kind of flood. I look over the heads of several people and something catches my eye. I suck in my breath, absolutely stunned. There, floating as calmly as can be in the water across the river from me is my little boy! He smiles his big smile at me, and I can hear his voice as if he is whispering right into my ear. He says, "Don't be afraid, Mother! You see? I am always here!" The river becomes calm, and I lay my head back in the water and just float, completely relaxed. I am no longer afraid. Finally, I awaken.

My Interpretation of God's Message

My first thought upon awakening was that I was exhausted. There was great terror in the dream, balanced by the assuring, calming influence of the child. As I began to think about the dream, I puzzled over the comment by the child that "my father is the sun." Then it hit me with a force that took my breath away. Not the sun, but the *Son*! I realized that there was powerful imagery at work here: stars of terror raining from the sky, a pregnancy and birth of a child, the sun, the night, a large lake and a raging river. So much of this dream was left unexplained, so I laid it aside for many years, trusting that it was a sacred message from God that would be revealed in his own perfect timing.

Okay, the laundry cart. I know exactly where that image came from, and I would not consider it at all biblical. When I had this dream, I was working for a hospital system in Ohio, and a seriously unenlightened administrator decided to give me an office in the basement of one of the hospitals in the laundry department. Some days, I literally had to climb over mountains of bags of dirty hospital laundry in order to get into my office. Apparently it caused enough stress to make its way into my dream. Enough said.

Fifteen years passed, and my husband and I moved to Houston. In an effort to meet some Christian friends, I joined a Disciple Bible Study at a church near our home. While reading my homework toward the end of the thirty-four week study, I turned my attention to Revelation 12. After reading a few verses I had a funny sensation that I had seen this material before. Strange, since this was the first time I had read or studied the book of Revelation. As I read further into the chapter, it suddenly came back to me with such force that it downright frightened me. *This chapter was my dream!* I slammed my Bible shut and jumped up from the couch where I had been comfortably reading. I was actually trembling and had to walk away for a while to gather my wits about me and to muster up the courage to open my Bible and see what God was trying to say to me.

The authority of the Holy Spirit had now stepped in. To assist and further enrich my understanding of this vision, I was guided to other passages from Scripture as I read my Bible in subsequent studies or during my own times of private devotion. This process of revealing his message has taken many years, adding layer upon layer of enlightenment.

To paraphrase verses one through six of Revelation 12, a pregnant woman is in labor, and a dragon sweeps a third of the stars from heaven to earth with his tail. The woman gives birth to a male child, who is to rule all nations, but her child is caught up and taken to God and to his throne. The woman flees into the wilderness. She is protected and nourished there for three and a half years. Finally, in verses 15–16, "The serpent poured water like a river out of his mouth after the woman, to sweep her away with the flood. But the earth came to the help of the woman, and the earth opened its mouth and swallowed the river that the dragon had poured from his mouth" (ESV).

Returning to the symbolism in my dream, it begins with terror falling from the heavens. I have been surprised at the references to the "stars falling from the sky" that the Holy Spirit has revealed throughout the years. In Matthew 24:29 Jesus states, "Immediately after the tribulation of those days the sun will be darkened, and the moon will not give its light, and the stars will fall from heaven, and the powers of the heavens will be shaken" (ESV). Daniel 8:9–10 concerns prophecy about an evil king who threw some of the starry host down to the earth and trampled on them. Daniel 12:3 indicates that the starry host may refer to the righteous people of God. And then there is the verse in Revelation 12 that refers to a dragon sweeping stars from the sky. Revelation 12:3–4 reads, "And another sign appeared in heaven: behold, a great red dragon, with seven heads and ten horns, and on his heads seven diadems. His tail swept down a third of the stars of heaven and cast them to the earth" (ESV). My research indicates that the dragon and the third of the stars in heaven most likely refer to Satan and his fallen angels who were expelled from heaven. So interestingly, the image of the stars falling from heaven represents the two opposing powers of light and darkness: the beloved children of God, and the terror created by the followers of Satan.

The "woman" in Revelation 12 is considered to be the heavenly representative of God's people, first as Israel, and then as the Christian church—the followers of Christ. For me, the dream's most meaningful symbolism is the child. Without doubt, the beautiful child in my vision is Jesus, the One who watched over me throughout the events of my dream. By stating that "*my father is the sun*" Jesus claims his position as God Incarnate, "the exact imprint of God's very being (Hebrews 1:1–3 NRSV); The Word was with God, and the Word was God (John 1:1 ESV); And the Word became flesh and dwelt among us, and we have seen his glory, glory as of the only Son from the Father, full of grace and truth (John 1:14 ESV)." Jesus, born of (the woman) Israel, will rule the eternal kingdom of God. His promise, stated twice in my dream that "I am always here with you," completes the Holy Trinity with the promise and presence of the Holy Spirit.

God used the beautiful imagery of the sun in my dream to teach that the Father and the Son are the true source of Light, and that the Light will rule over the darkness. The sun and the peaceful lake are also symbols of Christ, as he is not only the Light of the world, but also the Living Water. "If anyone thirsts, let him come to me and drink. Whoever believes in me, as the Scripture has said, 'Out of his heart will flow rivers of living water' (John 7:37–38 ESV)."

The flooding, raging river that was carrying me away in its current represents a time of trial.

Knowing full well that Revelation is a book of end-times prophecy, I believe my vision relates to an ultimate battle between heaven and Satan with respect to the salvation of the beloved children of God. Many scholars agree that Revelation was written during the time of great persecution of Christians during the Roman Empire. John, the author of Revelation, was exiled to the island of Patmos and wrote about his visions while in exile. Certainly, the persecutions of Rome were foremost on his thoughts, and I understand that Revelation was written with this in mind to give hope and courage to his fellow brothers and sisters in Christ. However, I believe that scripture is living and God-breathed, and that the visions John had both included and went beyond his era into the future. If Revelation was only about events that happened two thousand years ago, then God would not have sent me this dream vision in *my* lifetime. Again, God is the God of past, present and future.

I believe that Satan and his angels, those that were swept from God's presence in heaven, have been wreaking havoc on humanity for centuries, and that he plans to unleash great terror upon the children of God in the future. Something is coming. What form it takes remains to be seen. It could be a natural disaster or a terrifying war. It also could come in the form of an evil kingdom or regime. Regardless of the cause, history shows that in the wake of terror, chaos and confusion reign for a time. What better environment for Satan to emerge full force than when we are in the midst of chaos and confusion?

One of the most important lessons I have learned is that the book of Revelation, with all of its symbolism and apocalyptic literature, is in reality a book of hope and victory, just as John meant it to be. God wins! And in my vision, God gives his assurance that he is with us no matter what trials we face, personal or worldly, now or in the future. He is in control. In the midst of chaos, danger, confusion, or disaster, regardless of natural, man-made, or supernatural origins, Christ is there with us and for us, just as he was there floating in the raging, flooding river with me.

I was particularly moved by a striking message of love for the nation of Israel and the Christian Church, represented by the woman in my dream. From Genesis to Revelation, God has faithfully and consistently preserved a remnant of the tiny nation of Israel, and later, the Christian church, to persevere against several millennia of trials, exile, and incredible horrors, and that gives me great hope for all of us, *the starry host*, beloved of God! The child's gentle smile and loving words of assurance whispered to his mother as she is caught in the raging flood of my dream, "Don't be afraid, Mother! You see? I am always here!" touched me deeply. What a beautiful expression of God's love for Israel and for his Church!

One Thessalonians 5:2–11(ESV) poignantly relates to the events in my dream: "For you yourselves are fully aware that the day of the Lord will come as a thief in the night. While people are saying 'there is peace and security,' then sudden destruction will come upon them, as labor pains come upon a pregnant woman, and they will not escape!" I was surprised to discover that the term *pregnant woman* was defined in my Bible footnotes as a common prophetic expression for the suddenness of the day of the Lord! Thessalonians continues, "But you are not in darkness, brothers, for that day to surprise you like a thief. For you are all children of light. So then let us...put on the breastplate of faith and love and for a helmet the hope for salvation. For God has not destined us for wrath, but to obtain salvation through our Lord Jesus Christ." This portion of Scripture beautifully captures the roles represented by light and darkness in my dream.

I have new eyes as I look at the world I live in today and see the hatred and violence that fills the daily television news screens, because I know there is only one place in which I can place my hope. I enthusiastically join John in his eloquent plea at the very end of his book of Revelation: "Come, Lord Jesus!"

As I finished speaking, I realized that my eyes were squinched tightly closed and that I had been watching the vision replay in my mind as I told my story to Margaret. Again, I experienced the fear of the dream balanced by the peace of the presence of Jesus.

Without removing her hand from my shoulder, Margaret spoke to me in her now commanding voice. "This is a powerful vision that our Lord has shared with you my child. You have thoughtfully laid out your interpretation of its symbolism and implications. Now I want you to summarize the overall message God intended for you in this dream."

I kept my eyes closed and continued to watch the images of my dream flash in front of me. As I watched, a message unfolded.

"Treasure of my heart, I have revealed myself to you as Father, Son and Spirit, and I want you to know that I am here with you always. Do not fear the future and the trials it will bring. Because you believe in me, I am forever your Deliverer. Hope and Victory abide in me."

The Table Is Set

Behold, I send an angel before you to guard you on the way and to bring you to the place that I have prepared. Pay careful attention to him and obey his voice...

Exodus 23:20–21 (ESV)

Margaret strengthened her already-firm hold on my shoulder, her grip like an anchor, keeping me focused and in my chair. I was so thankful for the protective cocoon she had built around us, for the winds had reached a howling pitch and the eerie black clouds continued to darken and swirl in the sky above. I swiveled in my chair to peer up at Margaret, and I saw—*Oh, my goodness!—I saw two faint outlines appear on either side of her...*very tall, silver-robed figures standing silently at attention.

"Whoa, Margaret!" I gasped, thoroughly shaken. "You brought *reinforcements?*" Even though the wind did not touch us, I still felt a chill go up my spine. Now I knew what she had meant earlier when she referred to me remaining "under *our* protective cover."

My wide-eyed expression obviously translated my thoughts because Margaret nodded and gave me a serious little smile.

"All three of us were with you in your next dream vision, Jenn. You will recognize my two companions as you work your way through the telling of it. They are mighty angels, dear child, but do not be afraid, for they were with you at the command of the Holy One, to provide assistance and guidance to you during your dream."

I looked up at these mighty angels, and as I did, they both slowly nodded their heads in confirmation of Margaret's words.

"Continue with your next vision, Jenn," said Margaret, "and take comfort in our presence."

I am sitting in the back pew of the darkened nave (main aisle) of a Gothic-style cathedral constructed of dark gray stone. I face the altar, and before it is the transept, a rectangular area that cuts perpendicular across the main aisle and projects beyond it on both the left and right sides. The transept gives a cathedral the shape of a cross. A brilliant white light, flashing like lightning, is emanating from the arched entrance of the chamber on the left side of the transept, and I can hear screams and terrible explosions coming from the chamber. As I continue to look toward the altar, three figures wearing dark hooded robes run from this terrifying chamber. Two of them continue across the main aisle and disappear into the dark, yawning void of

the transept chamber on the right. The third figure comes to a halt in the middle of the transept with the altar behind him. He turns, looks directly at me, raises his arm, and with a grossly gnarled finger points at me, and hisses "Don't you dare!" as if he is warning me not to come any nearer or to interfere. I am so frightened that I feel as though I am going to faint, even though I am sitting down. The evil emanating from him is tangible. I want very badly to wake up, but something makes me stand up and walk down the aisle in defiance of the hooded figure before me. This is in total opposition to my personality, which overwhelmingly prefers to avoid danger or confrontation. I am aware that what I really want to do is to run the other way. The figure hisses again and then runs through the archway of the right transept chamber, joining the other two. I continue after him, terrified, feeling as if I am being pushed from behind.

I enter the dark chamber and am immediately surrounded by the three hooded figures. As they tighten their circle around me, they growl and hiss and throw off their hoods. I am greatly dismayed to discover that they are demons. They are horribly ugly with thick green-and-yellow skin and are intent on doing me great harm. I frantically try to think of ways to repel them, and the only thing that comes to mind is to recite the Twenty-third Psalm. I begin to say it out loud, but only get through "The Lord is my Shepherd, I shall not want. He makes me lie down in green pastures..." At that point, I cannot remember any of the words that follow. I begin trying to wake myself up, because I know I am dreaming and that if I do not wake up, these demons are going to get hold of me. Suddenly, there is a whisper in my ear. "Say the Lord's Prayer—you know this!"

So I begin to shout the words as the demons circle ever tighter around me. "My Father, who art in heaven, hallowed be thy name! Thy kingdom come, thy will be done, on earth as it is in heaven!" Suddenly, with the words "thy will be done on earth as it is in heaven," the demons stop their advance on me as if repelled by an invisible force field and completely change their appearance. The demons are gone, but instead, standing around me are three young adult men who appear to be of Middle Eastern descent. They look at me with shocked, confused, terrified expressions, and then run away from me deeper into the chamber. They are gone!

Feeling safe at last, I leave this chamber and walk back to see what is going on in the brilliantly lit chamber on the left side of the aisle, from which the demons had run at the onset of my dream. As I approach the archway, I notice that the screams and sounds of explosions have stopped. It is eerily quiet. Also, the formerly brilliant white light is now very subdued and has a reddish cast to it. I walk into the chamber and am dismayed by what I see. There are huge mounds of broken concrete and twisted steel everywhere. Clouds of smoke drift in the air. I do not see any people. As I slowly pick my way through the rubble, I realize that I am not alone. Two very tall figures are walking by my side, as if escorting me. All I can see is their robes that silently sweep the ground as they walk. I sense a quiet peace and reverence from them. As we walk through the rubble, I come across a Bible lying on the ground. I pick it up and dust it off. As I look farther ahead, I also spy a small red book. I walk over to pick that up as well. It is a Quran. I dust it off and carry it along with the Bible. Farther on, I see something blue and gold half buried by a chunk of concrete. We walk over to it and I pull it from the rubble. It is actually two items, a blue book with gold scrollwork on the front, and a type of stole that is also blue and has gold scrollwork that matches the book. A sense tells me that it is a copy of the Hebrew Torah and a vestment. I add these to the other two books that I have found. Suddenly, up ahead in the midst of the debris, a small round table appears, covered with a white linen tablecloth. I think that it curiously resembles some kind of altar. I am led to this table by my quiet escorts. There, I laid all the items that I have retrieved from the rubble. The three of us stand there silently, waiting. Then from up above, way above us, comes a loud voice that is so incredibly sad that it cuts like a sword to the very depths of my soul. The voice says, "The demons are killing my children!" With that, I am released and finally awaken.

My Interpretation of God's Message

I had this dream vision in November 2000, just before the Christmas holidays. My first recollection upon awakening was the knowledge that the voice I heard was God, and that he was grieving terribly. For several days, I experienced residual feelings of fear and dread and could not shake the profound sadness of the voice at the end of my dream. Since I had no immediate clear understanding of this dream vision, I let these thoughts, impressions, and feelings simmer and settle into my soul until God was ready to reveal his message to me. And reveal he did nearly one year later—in a big, and terrible, way.

On the morning of September 11, 2001, I sat in horror along with the rest of the country and watched as terrorists slammed their planes into the World Trade Center towers in New York City and the Pentagon in Washington, D.C. Sadly, a fourth plane crashed into a Pennsylvania field, thankfully missing its target because of its heroic passengers. Thousands of innocent people were killed, and we later learned about the Islamic fundamentalist organization, Al Qaeda, who claimed responsibility for this horrific event.

As I watched the damaged towers finally and slowly fall into a heap of twisted steel, concrete rubble and smoke, my dream vision returned to me with the force of a whirlwind, constricting my heart and stomach so much that I could barely breathe. "Oh my Father," I wailed in stunned disbelief, "is this what you were showing me?" Needing to be with other believers, I called my church and learned that they were already planning a special service that evening for people to come to mourn and to pray. I went to church that evening and wept with others as we prayed for those lost and for strength and guidance for our country. It was then that I began to understand the inconsolable grief that I heard in my Father's voice in my dream.

Once again, the authority of the Holy Spirit settled on me and began to provide insight into the images of my dream. To begin with, my dream opens as I sit in the back of a cathedral, observing the two chambers on the left and right. The chamber on the left side was full of light; the chamber on the right side was a dark void—another heavenly reminder about the ever-present war between the spiritual realms of Light and Darkness. My seated position in the back of the cathedral represents complacency. The demon running from one chamber to another, stopping to challenge me not to interfere, struck me hard. It is so easy in today's troubled world to ignore the atrocities going on around us, to say "there isn't anything that I can do about it." The insistence to interfere and pursue the demon in my dream (the pushing me from behind) came not from me, but from angels sent by my Lord. *My active involvement as a believer was crucial to defeating the power Satan had over the situation.*

As I entered the dark chamber and was surrounded by the three demons, I tried to say the Twenty-third Psalm, but couldn't remember the verses in the correct order and got confused. I have often wondered why I even tried to recite that Psalm in the midst of my terror. I have heard it many times in my life but have never completely memorized it. It does not at all seem the first thing that would jump into my head in a time of duress, yet it did just that. There is a reason for that, which I will share in a moment. Instead, I was directed by an angel to say the Lord's Prayer. The Lord's Prayer came from the lips of Christ Jesus himself as he taught his disciples to pray in Matthew 6:9–13. The words "thy kingdom come, thy will be done, on earth as it is in heaven" are heaven-sent and harness the power of the Almighty. The moment that I spoke those words aloud in my dream, the power of the enemy was broken, and the demons fled, leaving three stunned men in their wake. The sovereign power of the Almighty repelled the demons and, in his great mercy, freed these young men who had let evil into their lives. Even the demons know and recognize God. "And whenever the unclean spirits saw him, they fell down before him and cried out, 'You are the Son of God'" (Mark 3:11 ESV). The words of Jesus Christ carry incredible power, and when spoken aloud in his name can defeat our enemies, our oppression, and our fear. "Out of my distress, I called on the Lord; the Lord answered me and set me free" (Psalm 118:5 ESV).

To establish God's will on earth as it is in heaven is a powerful message. I can think of nothing more important for our earth and for our humanity than God's perfectly unfolding plan to establish his eternal kingdom among us. So now, whenever I pray the Lord's Prayer, I try not to say the words automatically. Instead, I slow down and let the words sink deeply into my heart.

During the days that followed the September 11 tragedy, I watched as a nation and world came together in grief and prayer. A memorial service was held at Ground Zero, the site of the former twin towers of the World Trade Center. Representatives from Christianity, Judaism, and Islam were present together on the stage for the memorial ceremony. As I watched the ceremony, my thoughts returned to the altar table in my dream where I laid the Christian Bible, the Islamic Quran, and the Hebrew Torah. And the voice, which exclaimed with infinite sadness, "The demons are killing my children!"

As I have considered the meaning of these images throughout the years, the impressions and words that come consistently to me are "children and mercy." The three books placed on the table represent people, and there is a tremendous need for healing to occur between the peoples represented there, including healing in their relationship with God.

God created human beings to be in relationship with him, and this relationship is a free will choice that each of us must make. This is a crucial choice. With whom will we align ourselves? Will we choose to be the beloved children of God, of the Light, or will we choose to be the children of darkness? As the events of September 11th have demonstrated, a frightening faction of the people of the Quran has chosen darkness, which has resulted in the shedding of precious human blood, and this grieves God terribly. And worse, these lost souls repeatedly invoke the name of "God" to justify their violent actions. Al Qaeda, this radical faction of Islam, has made very clear their intent to annihilate the people of Christianity and Judaism. This type of extremism is very dangerous and has been the cause of unspeakable terror and anguish in our world throughout the centuries. Those that practice this kind of hatred do not represent the righteous and beloved people of the one true God. Instead, they represent the enemy of God. And one day God will bring judgment upon the enemy and those who choose to follow him.

Now, here is where the Twenty-third Psalm fits in. Curious about why I tried to quote this Psalm in my dream, I took a long look at it, and suddenly verse 5 jumped out at me as if on fire. It says, "You prepare a table before me in the presence of my enemies.

You anoint my head with oil; my cup overflows" (ESV). *Matthew Henry's Concise Commentary on the Whole Bible* says the following about this verse: "The Lord's people feast at his table, upon the provisions of his love. Satan and wicked men are not able to destroy their comforts, while they are anointed with the Holy Spirit, and drink of the cup of salvation which is ever full." This is a powerful message. In my dream, the three books were the only objects left intact and rescued from the rubble of destruction created by the demons. I placed them together on the table provided by God. I think about the peoples represented by the books placed on the table, immersed and soaking in the almighty anointing of the Spirit of love, healing, forgiveness, mercy, and salvation. In the aftermath of terror, this table of healing and salvation is offered by God to all those affected by the powers of darkness. What a precious offering that is!

The great I AM offers this table because he is not only a God of judgment. He is also a God of mercy. In his unfathomable mercy, God has provided a way for those lost to darkness to find their way Home. That way is Jesus. Jesus, the overflowing cup of salvation, was sent to restore mankind to God.

Redemption is a theme found throughout the Bible, from Genesis to Revelation. From the redemption of Israel to the redemption of mankind, God is a restorer of relationship. The choice is open to us. Those living in darkness have an important choice to make. A fully repentant heart and acceptance of the gift of salvation that Jesus offers will restore a lost soul to God. Jesus changes hearts and restores relationships. Jesus said, "I am the way, and the truth, and the life. No one comes to the Father except through me" (John 14:6 ESV).

As he prepared to ascend to heaven after his resurrection, Jesus gave his disciples one final instruction, known as the Great Commission: "All authority in heaven and on earth has been given to me. Go therefore and make disciples of all nations, baptizing them in the name of the Father and of the Son and of the Holy Spirit, and teaching them to obey everything I have commanded you. And remember, I am with you always, to the end of the age" (Matthew 28:18–20 NRSV).

What a beautiful promise and what a blessing this Commission is to the people of the world who do not know God! Not just Christians, Jews, and Muslims, but people from every nation, tribe, and language. I am painfully aware of how much the Sovereign God of the universe treasures each and every one of our souls. He wants all children to join him at his table! His mercy is extended to all who make the choice to come to the table and accept the ever-present cup of salvation. It is never too late to choose to be restored to God and consequently, to each other.

There is also a serious warning here: if we remove ourselves from the table because of hatred and violence toward each other, we fall prey to Satan and the power of darkness. God grieves terribly about the destruction and death unleashed by his enemy, and his judgment will be fierce upon those who insist on remaining under Satan's power.

It is imperative that we no longer 'sit in the back of the cathedral,' watching and doing nothing. As children of God and heirs to his kingdom in Christ, we need to come together and be active in using prayer and our gifts of the Holy Spirit to bring his love and mercy to all peoples of the world, and to use the power of his love to destroy the hold that the Enemy has over our lives.

As I finished speaking, Margaret's strong, clear voice rang out behind me. "You have only begun, Jennifer, to sense the immense power that believers—the children of God—have over the evil and hatred that exists in this world!"

"Oh, Margaret." I sighed with a heart full of emotion. "God surprised me with yet another remarkable revelation regarding the responsibility we have as children of the Light. This revelation occurred on September 10, 2011—just one day shy of the tenth anniversary of the 9/11 tragedy. I was once again in Maine and took the local newspaper down to the beach to read about the preparations for the next day's 9/11 memorial ceremonies. I turned to the religion section and was stunned by the photograph that was printed on the first page. It was taken by a photographer named Ira Block, and the picture was of an open Bible fused into metal that was found by a New York firefighter in the rubble of the fallen twin towers of the World Trade Center.

"Margaret, I was so overcome by what I saw in front of me. For these past ten years as I have struggled to gain an understanding of this powerful vision, the Bible and other books found in the rubble in my dream have served as important symbols that have helped me to discern God's message for me. But what God showed me that day on the beach was that the Bible in my dream wasn't just a symbol. *It was real!* There in front of me on the page of the newspaper, was a photograph of a Bible that was actually found in the rubble. And when I looked even more closely at the photograph, something extraordinary was revealed. *God left a message for us in the aftermath of the terror attack!* The Bible fused in the heart-shaped shard of metal was open to Matthew 5, where Jesus is giving his famous Sermon on the Mount. This page contains Jesus' teaching on the Law of Retaliation, and the Law of Love. Chapter 5 verse 43–44 states, "You have heard that it was said 'You shall love your neighbor and hate your enemy.' But I say to you, Love your enemies and pray for those who persecute you, so that you may be sons of your Father who is in heaven. For he makes his sun rise on the evil and the good, and sends rain on the just and the unjust" (ESV).

"This is a clear message to extend the love and mercy of God to those that are the most difficult to love. We have a responsibility to pray for those that hurt us, those whom have become lost in the darkness, so that their hearts might be changed and that they will repent and accept the mercy and salvation so freely offered."

"Oh, my child," said Margaret softly, "God has honored you with this precious revelation. He is encouraging you to continue to trust him in increasingly deeper levels. Listen to him, dear girl, and he will continue to delight you with profound insights into his Word." She glanced over at the two angels standing in attendance beside her. "This extraordinary dream was full of revelations, and as participants in it, my companions and I are curious: What was the most meaningful message that God revealed to you?"

I closed my eyes and just let the words come, since they were already written on my heart. This one nearly moved me to tears:

"I have prepared a special place for you at my table, precious one, where you and any you invite can rest in my eternal promise of mercy, love and salvation. Beware of embracing hatred, because it will remove you from my table and from my protection. That, my love, would cause me unbearable sorrow."

Rainbows and Roses

Don't let your hearts be troubled. Trust in God, and trust also in me. There is more than enough room in my Father's home. If this were not so, would I have told you that I am going to prepare a place for you? When everything is ready, I will come and get you, so that you will always be with me where I am.

John 14:1–3 (NLT)

And this is the promise that he made to us—eternal life.

1 John 2:25 (ESV)

I tilted my head back and exhaled a long, slow breath. The telling of these past two dreams had been both exhausting and exhilarating. Margaret's firm grip, still on my shoulder, softened as she gave me a gentle pat. The wind slowly wound down to a pleasant breeze, and the turbulence overhead parted and melted away to reveal a deep blue sky dotted with white, puffy clouds.

Looking up at Margaret I noticed more changes taking place in her appearance, as well as that of our two silent friends. Margaret's gown had turned from silver to a sparkling mix of sky blue and green, reflecting perfectly the sky and the treetops swaying in the breeze. Her shield was nowhere to be seen. Our other two companions were also transforming before my eyes. Their silver robes were now white as snow, glowing faintly as if lit from within. Their faces were shining so brightly that I could not quite make out their features. They both nodded at me and I instinctively knew that they were smiling.

"Our friends are soon going to return to their home with our Father," said Margaret softly, "but first they wish to walk about and enjoy your beautiful gardens." With a mysterious twinkle in her eye, she leaned in close and whispered in my ear, "Watch them closely as they depart!"

My heart was filled with love and gratitude for these two mighty, yet gentle beings because I knew that they, along with Margaret, had been the angels watching over me during my dreams. They helped me to remain asleep in order to dream and receive the messages my Lord had intended for me. They gently prodded and guided me down the aisle after the demon's challenge and prompted me in my confusion and terror to say the Lord's Prayer in order to break Satan's power. They were my quiet escorts as I picked the three books from the rubble and placed them on the altar table.

My eyes filled with tears as I thanked them. "You were there for me, and I cannot even begin to tell you how much that means to me. It is so comforting—and empowering—to know that you are there fighting for me even when I cannot see you. Our God is a mighty and wonderful God to provide the protection of his angels for the children he loves so much! I hope that I will see you again someday, so until then, thank you with all my heart, and may God bless you."

The angels nodded at me in unison once more and walked slowly out into the yard. As they brushed silently by me, I caught a whiff of the unmistakable scent of white roses.

Margaret and I stood and watched our companions slowly walk about the gardens, stopping to observe a monarch butterfly immerse itself in the deep purple blooms of a butterfly bush. In the hummingbird garden, they watched as a ruby-throated hummingbird zipped in and paused to sip sweet nectar from a sparkling red glass feeder. They wandered over to the statue of St. Francis of Assisi, and as they did so, one of our resident bluebirds swooped down to take a drink of water from the basket in the statue's arms. Finally, as they walked through the back of the yard toward a large boulder hewn from the rocky hills of northwest Texas, the most magical thing happened!

The angels began to disappear, but it seemed as if they were walking through a strange doorway. A shaft of light, like a vertical slit, appeared and immediately formed a brilliant rainbow prism that fanned out on both sides as they walked through. My breath caught in my throat as I realized that the intense colors in the prism were the familiar colors of the rainbow, *but also included colors that I had never seen before*! I passed my hand before my eyes, because I really could not believe what I was seeing! Yep, the colors were still there, and as the angels passed through this entryway, the prism folded around them, shrunk to a sliver of blinding bright white light, and then disappeared altogether. The bluebird that had been drinking from the St. Francis statue flew right through the space the angels had just departed from and landed on top of his birdhouse in the back of the yard.

"Oh, Margaret," I breathed, "how absolutely *beautiful*! The doorway to heaven cracked open for barely a second and the light just spilled out! I had no idea there were so many colors."

"That was a special gift our friends left you with, my child," said Margaret.

I stood there in amazement as I absorbed what I had just witnessed and a thought occurred to me. "When watering my gardens and the water spray hits the sunlight just right, a rainbow appears out of nowhere. I have often marveled that those rainbows are probably always there, but need just the right conditions to occur in order for them to be revealed.

"But—wow—what happened just now tells me that heaven is like the rainbows. God and our two angel friends just now chose to give me a brief, beautiful peek at a realm unseen by human eyes!"

"I have an idea, sweet girl!" said Margaret in a lively whisper. "Let's walk over to the spot where they departed! Come!" Motioning with one hand to the back of the yard by the bluebird house, she picked up the hem of her gown with her other hand and began walking quickly through the cool grass. I joined her, and as we reached the spot where the beautiful prism of colors and shaft of light had briefly existed, I caught a slight lingering scent of the white roses. There was nothing left to see but my yard, just as it always had been.

Margaret stretched out her arms and began twirling slowly around. "Do this too!" she challenged playfully. So I stretched my arms wide and began twirling very slowly, secretly hoping that a neighbor would not choose to pick this particular moment to look out their window into my backyard!

"Now, Jenn, think about this as you gently cut through the air around you with your arms. Heaven is all around us, although with your earthly eyes you cannot see it. So right now, even as you are circling around in your backyard with your arms outstretched, you are embracing heaven at the same time!"

Okay, now that's cool! My heart began to beat a little faster as I tried to grasp the concept of embracing heaven. Oh, how I wished I could reach out with my wide open arms and give Jesus a great big hug! I lifted my face toward the warm sun, closed my eyes, and kept twirling. When I began to get a little dizzy, I stopped and opened my eyes. Margaret had already stopped twirling and was watching me with a look of pure delight. I could sense another important message coming my way.

"Dear child," said Margaret, her voice just above a whisper, "heaven has always been a great mystery here on earth. I know that you have been given a few precious glimpses into some truths about heaven, and

I want you to tell me about them in a little while. Our angel friends gave you this parting gift for a reason. Our Father wants you to know that the glimpses and little moments of truth that you have received about heaven are real and are from him. He encourages you to share what he has permitted you to see, because he knows that it will bring great joy and peace to those who have eyes that are open to see, a mind willing to accept, a heart tuned to the Word of God, and arms prepared to embrace joys that cannot even be imagined."

Margaret suddenly began fanning herself with her hands, making her soft white hair dance in wisps around her face. "Whew! My goodness, it is really getting warm out here! Let's get something cool to drink and return to our spot by the garden. Then we can speak more of heaven."

I left Margaret sitting out under the umbrella as I went inside to fetch some tall glasses of ice cold water. "Welcome to warm and humid Texas, Margaret!" I teased, as I set our frosty glasses on the table. "It has taken a while to get used to, but now I love it, especially how the air feels lazy and soft."

"Mm." Margaret nodded as she sipped her cool drink. Large beads of condensation trickled off the end of her glass and plopped onto her gown. They went unnoticed as she peered intently through the gardenia bushes planted in the garden next to us.

"Jenn, what is that sweet little plaque resting against the bottom of one of the columns?" she asked.

"Oh," I sighed wistfully, "that is a memorial for my little dog Mia. She was hit by a car several years ago and died. It completely shattered my heart. I loved her so very much. She always liked to roam about the yard sniffing the flowers, so I thought it would be nice to put a memorial for her in my garden…I call this Mia's garden."

"Do you believe Mia is in heaven?" asked Margaret.

"Oh, of course, Margaret, I absolutely do," I answered without hesitation. "My pets are such an important part of my life. They have always provided me with unconditional love and comfort, which are characteristics of the Creator himself. I have no doubt that God sent them to me and that, when they die, he takes them home to wait for that happy day when we will be reunited." I paused for a second, and then added timidly, "I actually had an encounter with what I believe to be angels the day after Mia died."

"Tell me," Margaret prompted gently.

"Well, Guy and I were so devastated by Mia's sudden death that we hardly knew how to function. The day after she died, we decided we had to get out of the house and go do something, so we put our other little dog, Isabel, in the car and we drove down to Galveston Island, which was a favorite place to take the dogs for walks on the beach. Tears streamed unchecked down my face as we walked along the beach, thinking about how much I missed my little Mia. Finally the tears subsided, and we took some comfort in watching Isabel happily chasing after little sandpipers near the water's edge.

"Suddenly, we came upon two men who stopped us and asked us about Isabel. They asked if she was an Italian Greyhound, to which we answered yes. They went on to say that one of them had had an Italian Greyhound that had been hit by a car and killed, and how difficult that time had been for him. I was stunned. We had not even mentioned our Mia, that she was also an Italian Greyhound and had been struck and killed by a car just the day before. As we talked with the two men about Mia and our similar circumstance, I felt calmed by their words and, for the first time since the tragedy, felt peace begin to creep into my heart. After a while they said their good-byes and walked away from us. We never saw them again.

"This was such an unusual encounter because people on the beach, upon seeing our dogs, usually said things like 'cute dogs…what kind are they?' and moved on. I am utterly convinced that the specific nature of this encounter can be nothing else but a heavenly intervention by angels sent by God to heal the broken hearts of two of his children that day on the beach."

"Oh, Jennifer, what a touching story! Our God is such a good and loving God! Your little Mia and all your other beloved pets are in his benevolent hands," said Margaret, her eyes misting with tears.

"Somehow, I know you are speaking the truth," I said with a tender smile. "I think of my sweet dogs and cats romping and playing together in heaven, in fields of green grass sprinkled with wildflowers and alive with butterflies. Cool shade trees line the bank of a nearby stream of clear, cold water, where they can rest and drink. That little 'mind picture' gives me great comfort and makes me smile.

"I love to hear what other people's 'mind pictures' of heaven are like," I continued. "When I was little, I thought heaven was a bunch of white clouds that you drifted on while playing the harp. It actually seemed pretty boring, except for the playing the harp part. One of my childhood friends told me that heaven looked like a gingerbread house—no...a gingerbread *city*— on steroids. It had buildings made of pearls, rubies, emeralds, and silver, streets made of gold and diamonds, and everything sparkled in a brilliant light.

"I have also heard heaven described as sitting in a beautiful garden with Jesus, an eternal church service, and a mysterious misty-looking place where spirits just kind of drift around."

At the mention of the drifting spirits, I heard another un-angel-like snort erupt from Margaret. She had her hands clapped over her mouth, but I could tell she was grinning. "That's a funny one!" she giggled.

"Well, I am relieved you think it funny, Margaret," I said, "because that means it is not so. Heaven is a very mysterious place to us humans, you know!"

"Yes, I do know," said Margaret, "and as one who resides in heaven, I am greatly enjoying this conversation. Tell me some more impressions that you have heard from those whom are close to you."

I thought for a second and then a bright smile lit my face as I recalled a precious memory of my mother's. "My mother shared an impression with me recently that she had of heaven as a little girl. It wasn't as much about heaven as it was about what happens when someone dies. She thought that when it was your time to die, a huge platform would be lowered from the sky by big ropes. You would jump on the platform and then be raised up into heaven."

"Oh, how darling! I love that!" exclaimed Margaret, clapping her hands, "her description reminds me of a giant swing!"

I nodded, smiling. "I like that one too."

"Now, dear girl," Margaret encouraged fondly with a twinkle in her eye, "tell me about your grandfather."

Oh! I was so surprised she said that! "I can't believe you know about that!" I gasped, "I keep forgetting you are an angel...of course you know! My very first, really serious glimpses into heaven, Margaret, came from my beloved Granddaddy Gordon, my father's father.

"Granddaddy Gordon and I had a very special relationship. We loved being together. We took walks, worked in the garden, and we talked about lots of things. He always told me he was proud of me, and that meant so much to a young lady who was very naïve and needed improvement in her self confidence. Granddaddy had a heart condition. If I remember correctly, he had what was called hardening of the arteries. He experienced several heart attacks before he died. Ten years before he died, he suffered a heart attack, but this time an amazing thing happened to him. He told me that when he had this heart attack, he was taken to a beautiful garden. He was standing at one end of a footbridge that crossed over a gently running stream. At the other end of the footbridge was a beautiful woman, dressed in white. She called him by his name 'Gordon!' and told him that he must not cross over the bridge to her because his time on earth was not finished. He so very much wanted to cross the bridge, but was firmly told no.

"From then on, Granddaddy told that story and talked fondly about 'his angel.' This was really big to me, because by that time, I was nurturing a deep, personal relationship with Christ, and I had often wondered where my beloved granddaddy stood with regard to God. He was raised in church, but something happened later in his life to turn him away. Thankfully, the loving influence of his second wife, Myrtle, led him back to his faith. It was so cool to hear him openly talk about his angel! I thought it was wonderful that God would nurture his beloved Gordon's renewed faith through a planned encounter with one of his angels.

"Ten years later, Granddaddy Gordon finally got to cross that bridge in the beautiful garden and returned home to his Lord. I was devastated, yet thankful for his presence in my life and that he was now home with my beloved Jesus. The one thing I did not expect was that my relationship with Granddaddy wasn't over. He had a very special gift of love to give me after he died. When we went to the funeral home for visiting hours the day before the funeral, I walked to the casket to see him. This is *not* my favorite thing to do, but my heart was broken, and I loved him so much that I wanted to see him one more time. When I looked at him, I was really taken by surprise. The man in the casket was not my beloved granddaddy. He looked like him, yes, but the essence, the person I knew and loved, was not there. That was the first moment in my life when

I realized, unequivocally, that *there is a soul*, and that when someone dies, it leaves and goes to a better place. That was my granddaddy Gordon's final gift to me. It was poignant, personal, and eternal. In fact, to preserve that moment in my memory, I took a small yellow rose from the spray that covered his casket and placed it in my Bible, so that whenever I came across it, even though it became brown and pressed flat, it would remind me of his precious gift."

I paused a moment to take a sip of my water while it was still cool—the ice was melting quickly. As I placed my glass back down on the table, I noticed Margaret was holding something in her hands on her lap. It looked—why…it looked like a yellow rose!

My dear angel friend reached out and placed the delicate yellow rose in my hand, folding my fingers gently around the stem with her own. I waited for the prick of the thorns and then realized that there weren't any. Margaret held my hand in hers and said softly, "This, Jenn, is a special rose, because it is from heaven. Take it and put it in your garden, and tend to it carefully, for it will grow and flourish. I want you to have something alive and beautiful to remember your special grandfather, for *just as the rose is, he is*."

Her last words flooded my heart with comfort. I brought the rose to my face and inhaled its wonderful fragrance; it was like nothing I have ever experienced before. I had a big lump in my throat and it was hard to get any words out, but I managed to nod and say "thank you" as I buried my face in the rose again to whisper a quick prayer of thanks to my Father in Heaven for this marvelous and precious gift. Then I carefully placed the rose in my water glass to sustain it until I had a chance to plant it.

When I regained control of my voice, I continued with my story about Granddaddy. "Granddaddy's story still doesn't end, Margaret! God has given me a spiritual gift that I cannot put a name to, and I know of many others who have experienced this same thing. Occasionally, while I sleep, I have experienced what I call visits from Granddaddy Gordon and several others close to me who have died. When I see Granddaddy Gordon, I walk and talk with him. We are always so happy to see each other, and he looks younger than I ever remember him. He seems to just 'check in' every once in a while.

"Another special visit was from a dear friend named Ed whom I met while working as a volunteer at a local hospital. Ed was seventy-three years old, and we were assigned to deliver lunches and flowers to new mothers. We became instant friends and shared many wonderful conversations. Ed had undergone extensive chemo treatments for cancer the year before we met and was in remission. But sadly, the cancer returned with a vengeance. At the end of his life, he was also diagnosed with ALS (Lou Gehrig's disease). It seemed particularly harsh for him to be suffering from two dreadful diseases at the same time. Though I only knew Ed for a brief period of my life, he held a very special place in my heart. Several months after his death, I had a dream visit from Ed. He was bathed in a beautiful blue light and he looked so well and happy. He grinned at me and said, 'They are working again, Jennifer!' and he wiggled his legs. In my dream I was confused and did not understand what he meant. Nevertheless we continued to talk, and then Ed told me that now that he had let me know that he was okay, I would not hear from him anymore, and true to his word, I haven't. When I awakened, I pondered our conversation during the visit, and then the realization struck me that Ed had been referring to regaining the use of his legs, which he had lost shortly before he died. With that wonderful realization, I was able to let my friend go, knowing he was renewed and happy.

"What I also realized was that during these and other dream visits I have experienced, there is an unmistakable sense of excitement in the air. As if those I am visiting with are waiting, in anticipation of something."

"What do you think they are waiting for, Jenn?" asked Margaret.

Without hesitation I replied, "I believe they are waiting for the return of Christ, when we will all be reunited with him in his eternal kingdom. When I see and experience the anticipation of those I have had visits from, it is most encouraging to know that even those gone before us know that there is something infinitely more wondrous to come!"

Margaret smiled. "Ah, my girl. That is a profound insight. Stop and take a minute to breathe in this truth. Breathe deeply and slowly and let it fill your spirit. Experience the anticipation of those gone before you and let it reside in you as well."

I did as Margaret directed and felt a quickening; a flutter of excitement that began in my heart and quickly spread throughout my whole being. I can only imagine the wonders that await us!

"Speaking of wondrous, Margaret, this has been an amazing day. Today I witnessed a dazzling display of color and light as our angel friends returned to heaven, and then I received this precious rose as a gift to remind me that Granddaddy lives in heaven. Both are startling in their testimony that the realm of heaven is present, active, and vibrant—as vibrant as those magnificent, breathtaking colors!"

"God has shared some precious glimpses of heaven with you, my child," Margaret agreed, her delight evident in those twinkling blue eyes. "And let me leave you with a thought about those breathtaking colors. The next time you see a rainbow in the sky, picture in your mind God cracking the door of heaven open, just a wee little bit, to look down and say 'I love you.' And as he cracks the door open, like he did today in your backyard, some of those magnificent colors spill out, forming the rainbow. God said to Noah regarding his rainbow, 'This is the sign of the covenant that I have established between me and all flesh that is on the earth' (Genesis 9:17 ESV). So every once in a while, our Father delights his earthly children by sending the rainbow as a reminder of his love, his promise and his presence."

"Now, *that*, Margaret, is the most beautiful description of a rainbow that I have ever heard!" My mind whirled with images of rainbows I have seen, and one in particular jumped out at me. "Hey! Guess what! I even have rainbows in my *hair!*"

My angel laughed her soft, musical laugh and nodded. "And?" she prompted.

"When I am out in the sun, sometimes the wind blows my hair into my face and around my eyes. The strands nearest my eyes become magnified, and I can see teeny, tiny rainbows dance up and down the strands of my hair. That has always intrigued me."

"It is no surprise to me, sweet girl," said Margaret matter-of-factly. "You have the very DNA of God in you because you are his child. *Of course* you have rainbows in your hair!"

I sat in amazement of that revelation and a smile slowly crept across my face. Margaret finally stood and stretched. "It is time for me to return to that beautiful place that I and many that you love call Home. Go happily about your day, sweet rainbow child, and I will return this evening. Tonight, I want you to share with me your dreams of death and heaven, for they contain powerful revelations. I guarantee it will be a very special evening!"

Before I could even manage a word of good-bye, Margaret faded into the sunlight; her blue-and-green gown shimmered and merged with the blues and greens of the sky and trees around us. Her familiar scent of white roses lingered behind.

I looked down at the table and the glass that contained the single yellow rose she had presented to me. Remembering her instructions to plant and care for it, I picked it up and found a perfect spot in my garden. I planted the rose, thanking God again for this special living gift to remind me of my granddaddy's life in heaven. I asked him to nurture and protect it, and to grow it someday into a beautiful rosebush.

As I dug in the soft, sandy soil, I could hear God's faint whisper of response to my prayer:

"I love to send you glimpses of your future, sweet child of mine. Your days on Earth are but an instant compared to the joyful existence that awaits you in my forever Kingdom. PS: I felt your embrace as you twirled in your backyard this morning. Thank you."

A surprised laugh erupted from me at those last words. Shaking my head in utter amazement, I stood, brushed the dirt off my knees, and went inside to tackle the large pile of laundry that had been waiting ever so patiently for my attention.

Death and Life

And the dust returns to the ground it came from,
and the spirit returns to God who gave it.

Ecclesiastes 12:7 (NLT)

Jesus answered him, "Truly I tell you, today you
will be with Me in paradise."

Luke 23:43 (NIV)

A chorus of tree frogs began singing their evening vespers as I walked outside to wait for Margaret's return. The air was considerably more pleasant now, and a soft breeze gently tickled my wind chimes. Shadows crept across the yard as birds busily scouted the last few bites of food before returning to the comfort and safety of their nests for the night.

As I stood quietly looking out at the backyard my gaze fell upon the yellow rose I had planted earlier in the day. I did a double take as a slight gasp escaped my lips. I had planted a single yellow rose, but there in its place was a small yellow *rosebush*! I shook my head slowly, smiling. God never fails to astound me with his glory and grace. Margaret was right. He so loves to surprise his children with gifts of love.

A soft giggle interrupted my thoughts, and I looked over to the chairs by the garden to see Margaret standing there. She was an ethereal vision of light. Her gown was a soft white, which shimmered with a radiance that cast a faint glow all around her body. I sensed that she had just come from the presence of the Holy Father himself and was still reflecting his glory.

"I see you followed my instructions regarding planting the rose, Jennifer!" she said, her eyes sparkling with joy.

I walked over to her and asked, "May I give you a hug?"

Without answering, Margaret reached out her arms and folded me into the most wonderful embrace. I leaned my head on her shoulder and just melted into the love and comfort that flowed out of her and into me. Wow, angel hugs are exquisitely delicious!

After a few moments she released me and motioned for us to sit down in our chairs.

"When I left you earlier today," said Margaret, "we were beginning to discuss your insights about heaven. Your next revelations are nothing short of little miracles sent to you from the realm of the Almighty. So now, sweet daughter of God, I want you to share with me your dream vision about the death of your friend Carol."

"Before I tell you about my vision, Margaret, let me tell you about Carol. I met her in choir practice at my previous church. Actually, I sat next to her. More often than not she closed our rehearsals with a prayer, and she prayed so beautifully and from the heart. I could tell that she had a very personal relationship with Jesus. I learned from others that five years earlier she had been diagnosed with and had undergone treatment for breast cancer, and was in complete remission. What a living testimony to God's healing and grace she was! Then one day, when it was time for our closing prayer, she asked if we would pray for her, because a routine cancer follow-up test was showing something that should not be there. As time went on, it became clear that the cancer had returned and had spread.

"Carol amazed me with her grace, her bravery, and her joy in the midst of her battle with this terrible disease. She seemed to care more for our grief than she did for her own, and she continued to offer her beautiful prayers in choir practice. She was determined to keep singing. She sang with us for our Christmas and Easter cantatas. Then the cancer spread to her brain and walking became difficult as it affected her balance. She began using a wheelchair and was not able to come to choir, but did come to church with her beloved husband, Robert, whenever she was feeling up to it. One of her goals was to finish her treatments and be well enough to sing with us again at Christmas. Our hearts broken, we knew that Carol's cancer was terminal, but we all prayed to keep her with us for as long as possible, and that she make her Christmas goal."

It is the night of June 13, 2005, when I have a dream about Carol. I am standing in a great hallway of an ornate old building. High arched windows run the length of the hallway on both sides, and smooth marble covers the walls and floor. The building has a museum feel to it and reminds me of photos I have seen of the New York City Library. There are lots of people walking the hallway in both directions, but no one I know. Then, the crowd parts, and I see Robert coming toward me, pushing Carol in her wheelchair. She is wearing a short white hospital gown. It looks as if she is 'holding court' as people are walking up and talking to her. I approach Carol, and not knowing if she can see or hear me, I say, "Carol, it is Jennifer." She replies, "I know, and I am doing a little better." Then I am pushed along in the crowd away from her. The hall suddenly becomes very quiet, and I realize that no one remains but me, Robert, and Carol. Carol rises up out of her wheelchair and says, "I have to lie down awhile. I am not feeling very well." She walks over to a table I had not noticed before. It reminds me of a sturdy, wooden physical therapy table, and it is covered with a thick, deep cushion of sheep's wool. Carol lies down on the table and buries her face in the thick wool. As she settles into the wool, Carol begins to moan and then begins to scream in agonizing pain—soul piercing, terrifying screams that make me so frightened that I cannot move. My heart wrenches and I feel like I cannot breathe. I can only watch in horror, hopeful that the deep, thick wool will bring comfort to her, and am thankful that it is muffling her screams a bit. As I watch, 'others'—tall beings in white—appear and

along with Robert surround the table so completely that I can no longer see Carol. Then the tall beings in white do a curious thing. They begin slowly and deliberately waving their arms side to side above Carol, back and forth, back and forth, as if they are somehow ministering to her. Carol's screams become muffled and quieter. Finally, the screaming stops altogether. The tall beings part and step back from the table, and Carol raises herself up on her hands and knees, crawls backwards and steps off the end of the table. As soon as she stands up, three of the tall beings in white surround her, linking their arms with hers. They turn and walk slowly down the hall away from me, Robert, and the table. As she walks away, I notice that the backs of Carol's legs are a fiery, angry red. I wonder to myself if these red areas are where the pain has just left her body. As Carol walks away with her escorts, I know that she is okay now. I awaken, shaken, very glad it was 'just a dream.'

My Interpretation of God's Message

That next afternoon, I called the church office to collect any prayer requests that had come in for the intercessory prayer team, which I led. The church secretary told me that "prayers are requested for Robert and his family, because Carol passed away early this morning." I was stunned. It was not expected at all so soon, at least not by me. I could only groan with sadness. When I asked about what happened, the church secretary told me that "Carol had a great day yesterday but last night she went downhill fast. According to her husband, she was in incredible pain—it wasn't an easy way to go." She went on to say that Robert was home with her when she died.

After hanging up the phone, I sat in my chair for a long time. Tears came as I mourned this beautiful sister in Christ. I experienced several strong emotions at once: sadness, for the loss of Carol; distress, from having a dream that in every sense permitted me to witness her death; and peace, because I knew that Carol had been attended to by angels. They ministered to her pain and escorted her into heaven.

This was a powerful dream because I had never before been permitted to witness the process of death. The transition between earthly existence and heaven was absolutely seamless. Never once was Carol alone. Her family, friends and Robert surrounded her while she was still living and as she began the process of death, heaven's angels ministered to her and carried her through to the life eternal.

Perhaps the most poignant and meaningful part of my vision was the presence of the thick, deep cushion of sheep's wool, and that Carol laid down and immersed herself in its comfort. After several years of puzzling over its meaning, I finally received a marvelous revelation: the sheep's wool represented Jesus himself. It makes perfect sense. Jesus is the Lamb of God, the Great Comforter, the Great Physician, and our beloved Shepherd. Carol, during the process of dying, was able to lay her head down in the lap of her beloved Jesus. I can't think of anything more beautiful or comforting than that.

Several days later at her funeral, the choir sang one of Carol's favorite anthems, 'The Majesty and Glory of Your Name.' Carol usually stood next to me when we sang, and in her honor, her chair was left vacant and her choir robe was draped over the chair. It was an emotional time for all of us. After the service was over, someone asked me, "Did it kind of freak you out to be sitting next to Carol's chair and robe at her funeral?" My honest answer was no. I felt so privileged and humbled to know that during her funeral, I knew exactly where Carol really was, and that knowledge brought me great peace and strangely enough, joy.

It was now dark and the stars were twinkling overhead. A full moon was beginning its trek through the night sky and cast a bright bluish hue among the shadows that stretched across the yard. Margaret and I sat quietly after I finished my story about Carol. The moonlight seemed to increase the wonderful radiance of Margaret's glittering white gown.

After a while, Margaret said softly, "Joy was exactly what you should have been feeling, Jennifer, after this vision that God sent you. Carol was a beloved child of our Father, and he saw her through every step of the way Home. And I know you learned something important from this experience, my dear. What was it?"

As I thought about it I realized that, oddly enough, the concept of *joy* was key.

"Do not be afraid of death, dear child, for it is your way back home to me. I have commanded my angels to watch over you and you will never make the crossing alone. I await your return with great joy!"

A knowing smile spread slowly across Margaret's face. "Speaking of going home, I know that you had a dream about Carol in her new heavenly home," she continued. "Would you please share that with me now?"

I leaned my head back and gazed up at the stars and began to tell her about an incredible dream visit I had with Carol a month after she died.

I approach a charming, white cottage-style house with a large, inviting front porch. The air is pleasant and warm. As I begin climbing the steps to the front door, the screen door opens and there stands my friend Carol, wearing a cheerful red-and-white apron. Her curly, near–shoulder-length white hair dances slightly in the breeze, and her cheeks are a rosy pink. She has a fresh-baked-cookie smell about her. She looks wonderful and happy! She gives me a big smile and comes out to greet me. "Jennifer!" she says, her eyes sparkling with excitement. "I am so glad you came to see me! I have so much to tell you. Heaven is not what I expected—it is so much more!"

Carol tells me that heaven is not just a remote place away from earth. Heaven is everywhere—an unseen world that exists alongside ours. It surrounds us and moves with us each and every day of our existence on earth, yet we are separated by a barrier put in place by God. She tells me that he (Jesus) can cross over to earth any time he is needed. His angels can do the same. Their bodies are able to cross the barrier between earth and heaven, whereas humans, by nature of our sinful flesh, cannot. When we are set free in death, we can then cross the barrier into our heavenly home.

Even more glorious is the fact that there is a steady, continuous merging occurring between earth and the realm of heaven, as if the barrier is slowly thinning. God is establishing his kingdom in the hearts of believers— throughout the ages, one at a time.

I listen in amazement to all that Carol is telling me, and it resonates inside me as a mind-boggling truth. As I stand there on the porch, the images begin to fade and I awaken.

When Worlds Collide

Look! I am creating new heavens and a new earth,
and no one will even think about the old ones
anymore. Be glad; rejoice forever in my creation!

Isaiah 65:17–18 (NLT)

So we fix our eyes not on what is seen, but on what
is unseen, since what is seen is temporary, but what
is unseen is eternal.

2 Corinthians 4:18 (NIV)

It has been several years since I had this dream visit with Carol, and the images still spin in my head as I contemplate their significance in our world today: realms colliding, Jesus appearing, angelic interventions.

After a few minutes, Margaret quietly asked, "What are your impressions, Jenn, of this dream visit you had with Carol?"

"Honestly," I replied shaking my head slowly, "I feel blessed by what she shared with me. To begin with, since I knew that Carol was now Home, in my mind's eye I saw her in the delightful setting of a charming cottage-style home with a large verandah-style front porch, a type of home that is particularly appealing and comforting to me. And when she came out onto the porch to greet me, she was so happy and excited to share with me something that caused her great delight. As she shared her thoughts with me, I began to understand these concepts with a clarity I had not experienced before.

"Carol told me that heaven is everywhere, all around us. It makes me immediately think of that moment you and I had here in the back of the yard when we embraced heaven together." Margaret beamed, her eyes sparkling, and I continued.

"It makes sense to me, Margaret. I used to think of heaven as somewhere 'up there,' far, far away. In the very first chapter of Genesis it states that heaven and earth are separate, separated by a barrier put in place by God. And that is true. We cannot see heaven, and we cannot go there until we are set free from our earthly bodies. I still think of heaven as 'up' since anything not *on* earth is *above*. But I do not believe that heaven is far away. I have begun to sense the closeness of heaven due to the heightened spiritual activity occurring today on earth. Considering that heaven, though separate from earth, is everywhere helps me to understand that *God is everywhere*. He sees our actions, he sees our hearts, and he knows our minds. He is with us all the time. When we choose to be in relationship with God, he sends his Spirit across the barrier to live within us, to guide us, to be our Advocate and Comforter.

"And even though Carol did not mention it specifically, one of her revelations stirred a more profound awareness in me regarding the essential nature of *prayer*. She told me that our Lord can cross over to earth anytime he is needed. Our merciful Father provided his children with a powerful lifeline to heaven, in order that we may communicate with him, through prayer, across the barrier between earth and heaven. When we cry out to him, he can respond in an instant."

With a nod of approval, Margaret's tone became serious. "Communication is crucial to the success of any relationship, Jennifer, both here on earth and in heaven. Our beloved Heavenly Prince was in constant prayer during his time on earth. He knew the value of and necessity of prayer, because it was his lifeline to his Father and his true home. My child, *even though God is all seeing, he still wants to hear from you.* He wants to know about the desires, joys, and concerns of your heart, and he wants you to ask him for help, for blessings, for spiritual gifts. Because when you do so, you are *choosing* to have a relationship with him; you are choosing to grow closer to him, and to put your complete trust in the one who has loved you since the very beginning. *That* is what brings our Father immeasurable joy."

"I cannot imagine *not* talking to God," I said thoughtfully, "I talk to him all the time. I told you earlier how Billy Graham encouraged me to talk to God and how that changed my life. Throughout the years as I have grown into my relationship with God, I have experienced spine-tingling examples of God answering the prayers of his beloved. People have shared many powerful stories with me of his divine intervention when all they have done is ask with honest and believing hearts.

"And speaking of spine-tingling, I had a personal experience with prayer that I will never forget. I was working for a hospital system in Ohio when the Federal Building in Oklahoma City was bombed on April 19, 1995. It was a home-grown terrorist attack and it left the nation reeling. Our faith-based hospital had a sister hospital in Oklahoma City, where many of the injured were being treated and where many of the dead had been taken. In an effort to express our love and concern for our counterparts who were caring for the victims and their families, we posted a huge banner in our lobby to provide a way for our employees, patients and visitors to share their thoughts and prayers. The long banner hung for a week, and every inch was filled with written prayers. It was beautiful and breathtaking. One short prayer particularly touched my heart: 'May God wrap your hospital and all who are within its walls in his loving embrace.'

"Finally the banner was carefully taken down and rolled up, ready for its journey to Oklahoma City. I was asked by our administrator to take the banner over to the other hospital in our system, where the shipping would take place. My job frequently took me to this other hospital, and I had planned to go over later that day, so I carried the banner back to my office and set it in the corner up against the wall behind my desk.

"As I sat down and got back to work, I was continuously distracted by the feeling of a presence in the room. It was so strong that several times I swung around in my chair and looked toward the wall. I could see nothing but the scroll of prayers standing silently there where I had placed it. But each time I turned my back to it, the little hairs on the back of my neck stood on end. Someone or something unseen was there in the room with me. It was then that I realized that prayers truly have a life of their own. They are not just words written down on paper, or words casually spoken. Prayers are like living bursts of energy and are carried straight to the throne of heaven. Carried by whom? My guess is that angels help carry our requests to the throne of the Most High. I don't know the answer to that, but I do know that for the rest of that afternoon, *I was in the presence of something holy.* And I know without a doubt that God heard every single one of those loving petitions.

"I truly believe, Margaret, that, just as Carol said, when God hears our cries of prayer, he hears and he acts. Our gracious Father commands all under his authority to minister to his beloved children of the earth. A close friend of mine told me a wonderful true story about three friends—Jenny, Margie, and Gina— that is a testament to God's mighty response to the needs of his children.

"Jenny suffered from a serious chronic lung disorder, and one Friday night was hospitalized and comatose. Her daughter was advised that if things did not improve overnight, that the family should be called in. More than eight hundred miles away that same Friday night and early Saturday morning, Margie had been deep

179

in prayer for her friend Jenny. She was waiting until a little later in the morning to call Jenny's daughter for an update on her condition. Meanwhile, early Saturday morning, Gina, another friend, decided to stop in to visit Jenny in the hospital. Gina was a Christian, but was without a church home and was at a point in her life where she longed for a deeper relationship with God; she needed to take her faith to another level.

"As Gina walked into the hospital room, several miracles occurred at once. As Gina approached Jenny's bed, she was amazed to see an angel sitting at the head of the bed, stroking Jenny's hair! Gina knew instinctively that no matter what happened, Jenny was going to be okay. *God opened her eyes so that she could see.* Imagine the leap her faith took in that very moment! At this same moment, many miles away, a worried Margie couldn't wait any longer and decided to call Jenny's daughter a little earlier than planned for an update. When she placed her hand on the phone to make the call, Margie was overtaken with joy and a revelation that Jenny was going to recover. Laughing and with a huge grin on her face, she placed the call to Jenny's daughter and told her that she already knew that Jenny was going to be fine. And she was right! Jenny did indeed recover.

"In this story, our heavenly Father ministered to each of these three women *in a single instant!* He answered Margie's prayer, and he sent his messenger to comfort Jenny *and* to enrich Gina's faith."

"That is just the tip of the iceberg, my sweet child!" Margaret exclaimed, the radiance around her growing suddenly brighter. "The Almighty is so powerful and so generous with his grace that he can respond all over the *world* in an instant!"

I sighed and tipped my head back in my chair. What Margaret just said was pretty mind-boggling for a human brain to comprehend! I couldn't help but feel God's presence as I gazed up at the great expanse of stars, knowing that he created all of it. And as vast as the universe is, God cares enough to be available whenever we need him. Margaret's very presence sitting next to me here in my backyard is proof of that!

"A penny for your thoughts?" Margaret's question brought me back from my reverie.

"I am feeling overwhelmed by God's love and care for us, Margaret. When I visited with Carol in my dream, she had that same sense of excitement and anticipation about her that I have sensed in others I have had visits from. She knows that much more is going to happen in God's plan for us and for those in heaven. It is so exciting to know that we are part of a plan that is still unfolding, a plan that holds many wonders for us. Remember that feeling of excited anticipation I felt in my dream about being on a journey? That is the kind of feeling I am experiencing now, but this time I am not dreaming!"

Margaret laughed delightedly. "Believe it or not, Jenn, all of us in heaven are experiencing the same kind of excitement that you describe!"

"Oh, my angel friend." I sighed, gazing up at the twinkling universe. "I wish I had a telescope that would enable me to see much further into God's Creation— to see galaxies and far-off worlds. When I recall what

Carol told me about God establishing his kingdom in the hearts of believers, I imagine watching two worlds slowly merging together, like pictures I have seen from the Hubble Telescope. *That* would be amazing to watch!"

"We *are* watching it happen, dear one!" said Margaret with a mysterious smile.

Goose-bumps again! I grinned and continued. "I have to admit that the concept is fascinating to me, and still a little confusing. But I have read several things that have helped me to understand what Carol alluded to about the merging of heaven and earth.

"In the book of Revelation, John frequently refers to the new heaven and the new earth and describes his visions of them. He writes in Revelation 21:1–3: 'Then I saw a new heaven and a new earth…And I saw the Holy City, the new Jerusalem, coming down out of heaven from God…And I heard a loud voice from the throne saying, 'Behold, the dwelling place of God is with man. He will dwell with them, and they will be his people, and God himself will be with them as their God' (ESV).

"And in his book *Heaven*, Pastor Randy Alcorn refers to a statement made by theologian Anthony Hoekema, who writes, 'So heaven and earth, now separated, will then be merged: the new earth will also be heaven, since God will dwell here with his people.'

"What I am beginning to understand, Margaret, is that while heaven and earth are currently separated God is, at this very moment, establishing the heirs of his kingdom through Jesus, who dwells in the hearts of all believers. As beloved sons and daughters of the Father, we have the privilege and responsibility to share the good news of Christ with others so that they may be heirs to the kingdom with us. Matthew 4:17 states, 'From that time, Jesus began to preach, saying, 'Repent, for the kingdom of heaven is at hand' (ESV).

"And finally, at the appointed time that only the Father himself knows, Jesus will return to complete his kingdom. Sin and darkness will be defeated forever, the barrier that separates heaven and earth will be removed, and heaven and earth will be renewed and finally merged together. God himself will dwell among us and the merged new heaven and earth will glow brighter than the sun with the Glory of God. *God's will be done, on earth as it is in heaven.*"

"Ah, Jenn," sighed Margaret wistfully, "I am proud of you! You are *getting it!*" She shot me a mischievous grin. "You have mentioned several times about your 'visits' with people in heaven who seem to be waiting, anticipating something. You are so right. They are waiting and anticipating the very day you describe."

"I cannot wait to experience that glorious, monumental day," I replied thoughtfully, "and as I view my life with this future in mind, it changes my whole perspective of my journey here on earth—why I am here and where I am heading. *I believe the single most important action in my life is to develop an intimate, deeply personal relationship with my Father in heaven.* And the purpose of my life here on earth is to continue to deepen that relationship in every level of my being, in heart, mind, and spirit; to be a careful and considerate caretaker of God's Creation; to use the spiritual gifts he has given me; to learn right living from the words of his Holy Scriptures; to teach others about him; to listen to my heart and nurture the things that bring me joy; to serve others and to become a person that reflects his image. I believe we are all being trained for roles that we will have in the eternal kingdom. That fills me with hope and great anticipation regarding my eternal future!

"There is still much mystery, and there are so many unanswered questions about heaven, and how everything will take place as God's plan unfolds. These are things only God knows, and that is as it should be. But these visions I have had about Carol have given me confidence in the knowledge that God has us in his loving hands, he has a plan, and that something wonderful awaits us. That, my friend, is something I can trust in and live with!"

Margaret reached over and placed her hand gently on my arm. "How wonderful and how marvelous, Jennifer, that God sent these revelations to you through a faithful sister in Christ. Why he chose Carol to speak to you is known only to him. You never know where his next message will come from, but in his mysterious way, it will come in a form that is special and perfect, just for you."

"This was special and perfect," I agreed. "I adored Carol, yet never in a million years did I ever think I would have an encounter with her that would teach me such a profound message of hope. If I were to briefly sum up the message from God that Carol delivered to me on my last visit with her, it would be this:

"Open your eyes and see that heaven embraces you, my child. I am within you and all around you. I am so close that before you call, I will answer! The day is coming when we will live together in a glorious new place, more wonderful than you could ever imagine! Trust in me, for my faithfulness endures forever."

As I finished speaking, I felt a tingling sensation all over my body. I peered down at my arms and noticed that they were glowing just the slightest little bit. Then, my clothes began to glow. Startled, I looked over at Margaret. The radiance I had noticed coming from her gown and her body was now spreading over to me!

Margaret laughed her wonderful tinkly bell laugh, and said, "Don't worry, sweet girl, I thought I would share just a bit of heaven's glory with you. When I left you for a while today, I spent time with the Almighty in his throne room. The radiance you noticed about me comes from the reflection of the glory of God himself. Everything in heaven, Jennifer, radiates with the reflection of his glory—*everything*. And when God reunites all of us together in the new heaven and earth, there will be no need for sunlight, because we will be lit by his Almighty presence."

I smiled and hugged my arms to my chest, soaking in the glory of God that she was sharing with me. I did not want this moment to end, ever.

But end it did as Margaret stood and prepared to leave me for the night.

"It has been a long day for you, dear child," she said. "It is hard to believe it was just a few hours ago that our angel friends gave you a brief glimpse of the heavenly gateway as they left here to return home! We have covered a lot of ground since then. You must get some rest now."

Looking back on our day together, I could not believe how much had happened. It was uncanny how being with Margaret made time appear to slow down. Although completely exhilarated from experiencing God's glory, I realized that indeed, I was getting very sleepy.

"Okay Margaret." I yawned without squeaking! "Will you be here in the morning?"

"Oh, yes," she replied enthusiastically. "And I am looking forward to it already! I have become very fond of our poolside chats. Have the umbrella up for us. I have a feeling it is going to be another warm day! Good night, dear one. May Jesus give you a good rest."

And with that, she headed toward the St. Francis statue and disappeared, her soft glowing radiance slowly fading into the dark, leaving only the scent of white roses behind.

The Language of God

Suddenly, there was a sound from heaven like the roaring of a mighty windstorm, and it filled the house where they were sitting. Then, what looked like flames or tongues of fire appeared and settled on each of them. And everyone present was filled with the Holy Spirit and began speaking in other languages, as the Holy Spirit gave them this ability.

Acts 2:2–4 (NLT)

Refreshed by a wonderful night's sleep I awakened early, poured myself a cup of coffee, and sat at the kitchen table, savoring the quiet of the morning. Gazing through the window I could see that it was another beautiful Texas dawn. The sky was streaked with a pink blush and the grass glistened with dew. I watched with amusement three little juvenile bluebirds racing through the yard, playing a game of chase with one another. My husband and I have affectionately named these birds Larry, Moe, and Curly (of the Three Stooges) because of their funny antics. We have watched them leave the nest and learn the necessities of life together—flying, feeding, and most recently, how to drink and take a birdbath.

This morning, Larry, Moe, and Curly flew over to the tall, elegant Rebecca fountain in the back of the yard. Water gently gurgled from the top of the urn the graceful statue has hoisted on her shoulder. All three birds perched on the edge of the urn and took turns hopping into the water, merrily splashing their feathers. I grabbed my binoculars and walked out onto the back porch to get a better look. Now I could hear their sweet little chirps as they played in the water. A shimmer of pink entered my vision in the binoculars, and I lowered them from my face to see what had caught my attention. I could only smile and shake my head, because, of course, there was my lovely Margaret standing there by the fountain. She was truly a feast for the eyes this morning. Her gown was a perfect, cotton candy pink, capturing the pink blush of the sky, and it glittered and sparkled, creating the illusion of tiny little prisms that reflected the morning light. Oh, how I wish she could bring me a bolt of that fine fabric from heaven!

Again using the binoculars, I watched as Margaret raised her arms shoulder height and cupped her hands. Without any hesitation whatsoever, Larry, Moe, and Curly all hopped off the fountain right into her hands and sat there, twittering gaily at her. I could hear Margaret's merry laugh as she held the darling little bluebirds. They were so contented. It was as if they could sense their Creator in her presence. Then, with a gentle flick of her hands, she released them into the air, and they hopped back onto the fountain and resumed their splashy bathing ritual.

"Good morning, Jenn!" called Margaret cheerily as she began to walk toward me. I waved to her and put down the binoculars. Then, remembering her request before she left last night, I walked over to the garden table and raised the umbrella.

"Ah, what a glorious day the Lord has made." Margaret sighed as she settled into a chair. Her small, bare feet and the bottom of her gown were damp with dew. She looked at me prettily and gave me a smile that showed all of her perfect white teeth. "I will join you in a delicious cup of coffee, Jenn, while we still have the cool breeze of the morning upon us."

I grinned at the not-so-subtle hint and left the lovely vision in pink sitting contentedly under the umbrella while I went to fetch our coffee. As I opened the door to the house, Cody burst through, almost knocking me off my feet in his haste to get outside and say hello to his beautiful new friend.

When I stepped back out onto the porch carrying two steaming mugs, Cody was happily licking Margaret's hands and toes, his tail wagging back and forth at light speed. "Sorry for the doggy kisses, Margaret!" I called, "that is just Cody's way of saying hello!"

"Oh, it is a lovely way to say hello." Margaret giggled. "It tickles!"

I laughed with her and said, "Cody has a unique talent for communicating special things to people. He is kind of like Scooby Doo!"

"Scooby Doo?" Margaret asked. Then she held up a finger and said quickly, "Wait a minute!" then closed her eyes and sat very still for a few seconds. Suddenly, she laughed out loud and clapped her hands. "Ruh-rho! What a very funny dog Scooby Doo is!"

Wow, I thought, there must be an angel reference department for cartoons that she just tapped into. Very cool.

"So, Jenn, how is Cody like Scooby Doo?"

"Well," I replied with a twinkle in my eye, "Cody can tell you that he loves you."

"Oh, how fun!" Margaret laughed and clapped her hands again. "Show me!"

I pulled a treat from my pocket and gave it to Margaret. I instructed, "show Cody the treat and say to him, slowly and distinctly, I...love...you!" Cody sat expectantly in front of Margaret, and when she did as I had instructed, Cody cocked his head and said roughly in three distinct syllables, "Rhy Rhuv Rhroo!"

"Ooooooh! Good boy!" Margaret squealed in delight and gave Cody his treat. "That is wonderful! It must be very difficult for a dog to learn to say human words, and he did very well indeed!"

Margaret and I settled happily back into our chairs and watched as Cody raced off in search of squirrels to chase. We sipped our coffee and sat in quiet fellowship for several minutes, relishing the soft, cool breeze that we knew wouldn't last much longer.

I was the one who spoke first, breaking our quiet reverie. "You know, Margaret, watching you listen to Larry, Moe, and Curly's sweet chirps as they sat so contentedly in your hands, and then later as Cody told you he 'loved you,' I can't help but be reminded of one of my most precious gifts of the Holy Spirit. It is also the gift I have had the most difficulty speaking about."

"Ah," said Margaret knowingly, "I have wondered when you were going to get back to this topic. You mentioned it to me early in your story. I think now is as good a time as any to speak of it, don't you agree?"

"I guess so," I agreed with a sigh. Timidly, I looked down at my feet, and I could feel my stomach churn in anticipation of talking about something largely misunderstood by many people.

Margaret set her coffee cup down on the table, then reached over and took the cup out of my hands and placed it on the table next to hers. I got the feeling she wanted my full attention. She did. With her hands she gently tipped my chin up so that I was looking into her beautiful, wizened face.

I looked deep into Margaret's blue eyes and found courage there.

I spoke softly. "All those years ago, by the bedside in Michigan, at the moment I asked Jesus to come into my life, the first thing that happened to me was that I began to speak in tongues. It is an experience hard to describe, but every time I am moved to speak in the Spirit, it literally fills me to overflowing and it just spills out. I have guarded this gift carefully throughout my life and have kept it very private."

Still holding me fast in her gaze, Margaret asked, "Why is this gift so important to you, child?"

"It was the first gift of the Spirit that God gave to me, and it felt so intensely personal. Even though I did not know what I was saying, I felt that I was speaking in a language that only God could understand. I know that there are those who are gifted with the interpretation of tongues, but that was not given to me. Yet, it hasn't really mattered, because the most precious thing about this gift is that for me, *it is absolute proof of the existence of the Holy Spirit.* The Holy Spirit is real. The Spirit lives within us, and it speaks to us in that still small voice and through the many gifts God graces each of his children with. For me, speaking in tongues was just the beginning, for since the Spirit now resided inside me, just as Jesus had promised it would in those who choose him, all the other gifts we have been discussing followed."

"Oh, dear child, that is a marvelous truth!" exclaimed Margaret. "You must hold fast to that. Jesus's disciples received the gift of tongues during Pentecost, when the Holy Spirit came to man just as he had promised. This gift enabled them and others to teach the good news about Jesus to people of foreign tongues all around the earth."

"I have always deeply treasured this gift, Margaret," I assured her. "Even though I have come across people throughout my life who scoff at the gift of tongues. It has been hurtful to me to participate in conversations when the subject of the spiritual gifts comes up for discussion. I can feel my heart and spirit quicken as I think maybe, just maybe, I will be able to share my experience with this gift. But before I ever get the chance, someone will laugh at or criticize the gift of tongues, saying things like, 'It is all fake,' or 'I would never want that gift—it is too weird.' I find myself feeling humiliated and sad that I cannot speak of this precious gift without being ridiculed, so I say nothing at all. I am ashamed that I have not been a very good witness for my Lord."

"I am so sorry, Jenn," said Margaret softly, her eyes reflecting the disappointment that I felt. "Unfortunately, people criticize what they do not understand. And what they do not understand is that you, and many others, have been gifted with the ability to speak in the *language of God*. Listen to what scripture tells us: 'For one who speaks in a tongue does not speak to men but to God; for no one understands him, but he utters mysteries in the Spirit' (1 Corinthians 14:2 ESV).

"This, Jennifer, is an intensely personal gift and must be used wisely and with discretion. I know that you have learned much about how you can use your gift. Would you like to share that with me, or do you wish to keep it private?"

"I would very much like to share, Margaret," I said enthusiastically. "I have waited a long time to be able to talk about this with someone who wants to hear!"

I picked up my coffee cup and sat back in my chair, savoring the taste and aroma of the fresh, strong brew. I reflected momentarily about Cody saying 'I love you' to Margaret in his very best doggy language.

Then I began to share some of my most private thoughts with my dear angel friend. "What I sense, Margaret, when I am speaking in tongues, when the words are flowing from deep within me and pouring out through my lips, is an *ancient presence, a wisdom beyond my own understanding* and *pure, unconditional love.* I have only used this gift while in prayer. There are times when I am deep in prayer for someone, and am at a loss for what to pray for. I may be praying for someone who is dying, and I wonder, what should I pray for? Should I ask God for healing? Should I pray for God to take them home and stop the suffering? In situations like this, I let the Holy Spirit do the praying and give way to speaking in the Spirit. There is a scripture that is very precious to me that says, 'Likewise the Spirit helps us in our weakness; for we do not know how to pray as we ought, but that very Spirit intercedes with sighs too deep for words. And God who searches the heart, knows what is the mind of the Spirit, because the Spirit intercedes for the saints according to the will of God' (Romans 8:26–27 NRSV).

"This scripture has brought me such peace. There have been many times of heartache in my life when I have gone to the Lord in prayer, and all I could do was sigh. It has been so comforting at times like this to know that the Spirit knows my heart and knows even better than I how to talk to my Heavenly Father. I trust it completely."

I heard a little sniffle and looked over at Margaret, who was wiping away a stray tear that had begun making its way down her cheek. I knew that she understood completely the various heartaches that had prompted my sighs. She waved her hand for me to continue.

"I have an example about how the Holy Spirit intercedes that happened to me relatively recently. It is a wonderful combination of two of my gifts: a dream vision and an alert to prayer by the Spirit.

"My father needed hip replacement surgery, and I traveled back to Ohio to be there for him and for my mother. The surgery went well, and Daddy was to stay in the hospital for about three days. While I was in town, my sister asked me if I could stay at her house for a couple of days with their three children while she and her husband made a quick trip out of town to attend a charity event. Always happy to spend time with my nieces and nephew, I agreed, as long as my mother did not need me at home. Mother was spending most of her time at the hospital with Daddy, coming home only at night to eat and sleep, so she encouraged me to go spend time with the children.

"The first night at my sister's house, I settled into the comfy guest room bed and fell fast asleep. It had been a long few days. While asleep, I had a dream."

I am at my parents' home and the phone begins to ring. As I start to pick it up I see that the phone number showing on the screen is from the hospital where Daddy is staying. I try to answer but hear nothing. Thinking that Mother has picked it up upstairs, I go up to inquire if everything is okay. As I walk into her room, she is scurrying around as if getting ready to go somewhere in a hurry. She tells me that Daddy needs her right away, so she is going to go to him at the hospital. Next, I see Daddy in his hospital room, wildly thrashing around in his bed. Then Mother walks into his

room and crawls up onto the bed with him. At that moment he becomes calm, and my dream ends.

"I awakened with a start and reasoned that I was just experiencing a delayed reaction to the normal anxiety anyone would feel after having a loved one go through surgery. But the dream disturbed me. I tried to go back to sleep but had no success, which was unusual for me. I looked at the clock and it was 3:00 a.m. I had the feeling that something was not right and could not shake it. Finally, I began to pray, and after a while I just let the Holy Spirit pray through me in tongues, since I really didn't understand what was going on.

"At 3:30 a.m., I finally felt released from whatever was keeping me up and in prayer. I promptly fell back to sleep and slept soundly until about 8:00 a.m. I decided to call my mother at the house to check in with her before she left to go back to the hospital. She did not answer the house phone, so I tried her cell phone. Mother picked it up right away and spoke very softly, almost in a whisper. I asked her where she was and she told me that she was already at the hospital. Then she went on to say that she had received a call from my father in the middle of the night. He was having a bad reaction to the narcotics that he had been given for pain and was very agitated. He pleaded with her to come and be with him, so she got dressed and drove to the hospital and was there with him by 3:30 a.m.

He was finally calm and sleeping soundly after a new medication had been administered.

"I remember thinking, 'There you go again, God!' You would think I would be used to this by now, but episodes like this still fill me with awe. My Heavenly Father permitted me to have another dream vision and sent his Spirit to help me pray in the midst of this crisis my parents were experiencing. He let me know in no uncertain terms that while this event was being played out, *he was all over it.* He was there in the room with my daddy, he was there at the house with my mother, and he was at my sister's house with me. The Almighty's love and care for his children is powerful and ever-present."

Margaret clasped her hands over her heart and smiled her beautiful smile at me. "The Holy Spirit intercedes *according to the will of God.* God is good!"

"All the time!" I responded happily, feeling like a big weight had just been lifted from my shoulders. Concealing my enthusiasm and gratefulness for this special and personal gift of the Spirit for so many years has been a burden.

Just then, in a breathtaking display of brilliant yellow and black, a large swallowtail butterfly left the flower he was feeding from nearby and perched delicately on the rim of one of the coffee cups in front of us. His wings gently moved up and down as he watched us. Margaret laughed softly and raised her face to the sky. I thought I saw her mouth a silent "thank you!" so I peered around the umbrella and looked up to see whom she might be talking to. Of course, there was no one there.

"Margaret?" I began.

Margaret turned her merry eyes on me and said, "This, sweet girl, is a little gift for you from the Holy Spirit. Whenever you see this butterfly in your garden, he wants you to remember the transforming power of the Almighty and how his gifts can be used to transform the lives of his children. Let these words be written on your heart, '*To whom much is given, much is expected.*'"

"Just as the butterfly is transformed from a caterpillar into a beautiful creature, so *you* were transformed when you sought and accepted Jesus into your heart. And the gifts he gave you have empowered you to transform the lives of others. The type of prayer in the Spirit that you just described is a powerful form of intercession for others. Remember the dreams about your grandmother's fall and the baby with the heart condition? You have long wondered what you were supposed to do with that information. Now, dear child, God has given you your answer, and he has given you a job to do. You are to intercede with prayer when prompted by the Spirit."

I sat very still and realized that Margaret was absolutely right. I wished I could have realized that truth back when I had first experienced those dreams, so that I could have interceded in prayer for those I cared deeply about. I sighed with the acknowledgment that I really do sometimes take a long time to get it!

Margaret gave me a gentle smile, and I knew that she understood. "Learning to use God's gifts is a process, Jenn. You have been faithful in your desire to learn from him, and he has been faithful to you in return. Jesus promised to provide the Holy Spirit, the

Comforter, to his people once he had ascended into heaven. Can you describe to me what the presence of the Holy Spirit has meant to you in your life?"

For me, the answer was easy, because I had been harboring this truth for a very long time:

"When I promised that I would be with you to the end of the age, I meant it. To find me, look inside yourself. Call upon me, my beloved. I am always there."

Margaret smiled and said thoughtfully, "You are right, he *is* always there! And he has told you so several different times. Think back a minute. In the dream where you met Jesus, he held a candle for you and told you *I will always be here for you, Jennifer.* Then, in your dream about the beautiful child who was Jesus, as he waded into the lake he told you, *I am going to my father now, but I will always be near if you need me.* And again, in the same dream when he was floating across from you in the flooding river, he said to you, *Don't be afraid…You see? I am always here!"*

I gasped as a stunning message emerged that had been hiding away in my dreams until this very moment. This beautiful heavenly emissary sitting by my side had pulled these statements from my dream visions throughout various stages of my life and helped me see them together as one profound truth. *The Holy Trinity—Father, Son, and Holy Spirit—is with me now and forever. And the Trinity will remind me of that as many times as I need to hear it!* My knees felt weak as I let that sink in. *Does God still speak to us? Oh, he most certainly does!*

Margaret gathered me in her arms and gave me a warm, delicious hug. "Congratulations, my girl!

You have learned the lesson that our Father has been teaching you all along! The proof lives inside you in the many gifts of the Spirit he has provided. And he will keep providing as your needs and circumstances change. That is what is so wonderful about God—he speaks to us where we are in life. He will always give you what you need, when you need it." Then she said with a twinkle in her eye, "Just remember, his version of what you need may be very different from your own, so hold fast to the truth that you are his child and that he knows his plan for you. Trust in him always—it's worth it!"

Speechless, I clasped my hands to my heart and sat very still. Sensations of joy, tenderness, and awe swirled through me as I thought back over all that Margaret and I had talked about these past few days. The life experiences, the dream visions, the quiet voice of God, the gifts of his Spirit, all interwoven by a common thread—his patient and consistent message of unconditional love for me and for all his children.

I secretly prayed that I would remember all of this in enough detail so I could write my book, since it seemed that I now had everything I needed to begin writing. I could feel tears of gratitude forming as I realized that I could not have accomplished this task without God's help. What a wonderful gift Margaret has been to me!

Seeing big tears welling in my eyes, Margaret smiled in understanding.

"We all have much to be thankful for, Jennifer. We have a Father who loves us dearly! And I am so thankful that he has given me the privilege of being your guardian angel. I have so enjoyed watching you grow, recognize your gifts, and learn how to use them to bring glory to God. You will continue to learn, and I am looking forward to many more adventures together in the years to come!"

The thought of more adventures with my dear Margaret made me smile despite the tears.

Then Margaret's eyes suddenly lit up as if she'd just had a huge 'aha!' moment.

"Jenn!" she exclaimed, "We have so much to be thankful for that I think it calls for a celebration! Oh yes! That is exactly what we need!"

She clapped her hands together, bounded out of her chair, and practically skipped to the edge of the patio, where she stopped, hands on hips, and stared out over the backyard.

I watched her, mystified. I could tell she was in big-time planning mode.

Margaret finally turned and faced me, her face glowing with excitement. "Remember the wonderful garden party you had to celebrate your birthday, Jenn?"

"Of course I do, silly"—I laughed—"it was the party I had always dreamed of!"

"Well then, dear child, you are in for a double treat, because tonight we are going to have another party right here in your own backyard gardens!" Margaret gleefully clapped her hands. She was positively quivering in anticipation. "I am going to have to leave you for now, because there is much to do to get ready. Look for me here after the sun goes down. *Oh, Jenn! We are going to have such a special evening!*"

I shook my head and giggled. It tickled me to see her so obviously excited. I managed to call out "Okay, Margaret, I will see you tonight..." just before she shimmered and disappeared into thin air.

I stood up from my chair and looked out at the yard. A garden party hosted by an angel. That sounds, well... heavenly! Margaret's enthusiasm was catching, because I began to feel the tickle of anticipation butterflies fluttering around in my tummy. I gathered up our empty coffee cups from the table and headed inside. Halfway to the house I stopped dead in my tracks and sucked in my breath.

"Oh my goodness gracious!" I exclaimed aloud to myself. "What in the *world* am I going to *wear?*"

Garden Party

Awake, O north wind, and come, O south wind!
Blow upon my garden that its fragrance may be
wafted abroad. Let my beloved come to his garden
and eat its choicest fruits.

Song of Solomon 4:16 (NRSV)

After an interminably long day anticipating what was certain to be a wondrous evening, I finally walked to my closet to pick out something to wear. I still had not made up my mind. What does one wear to a party hosted by an angel? Casual? Dressy? As I snapped on the light, I gave a slight gasp. My decision had already been made for me! Hanging prominently on a hanger before me was a beautiful pink dress that shimmered and glistened in the light. It was a simple, yet elegant three-quarter–length dress with long sleeves, a fitted bodice, and a slightly flared skirt. With elation I realized that the fabric was the same as that of Margaret's gown, which I had admired so this morning! I quickly slipped on the dress. Of course, it fit perfectly and made me feel like a princess. For my feet, I chose pink sandals that my young niece calls my Barbie shoes.

The sun had set and darkening shadows had begun their nightly trek across the lawn. I was so excited I could hardly bear it. I peered out the back door every minute or so, hoping to witness Margaret's return. Thirty minutes passed and still nothing. It was now dark. The night air was still quite warm, so I slipped into my bedroom one more time to pin my hair into a soft updo. Finally satisfied, I walked back through my room, and my eyes caught a glimmer of something bright through the plantation shutters on the windows. My breath caught in my throat as I hurried through the house and stepped out the back door onto the porch.

Words can hardly describe the vision that my eyes beheld. My backyard was completely transformed! All around the pool, on the patio, on the grass, and around the fire pit stood enormous white rosebushes. They glowed with an ethereal white light and floating above and around each rosebush were several glowing white orbs, similar to votive candles. They slowly circled and danced among the roses, creating the most beautiful visual effect I have ever seen. The very air was tinged in a white luminescence and was saturated with the fragrance of the white roses mixed with sweet almond and night-blooming jasmine from my gardens. Intoxicating!

As I stood there marveling, the space around my statue of St. Francis began to glow with the same ethereal white light. Margaret appeared first. She was dressed in a lovely white gown, which sparkled like new fallen snow in the moonlight. Around her waist she wore a loosely tied scarf that looked as if it were made from spun gold. I don't think I have ever seen her look more beautiful than tonight. As she stepped from the garden, two more angels appeared, dressed in the same sparkling white gowns, but these angels wore great spun gold sashes across their chests. They were tall and handsome, with dark brown hair and radiant faces. My heart leapt for joy as I recognized them—they were the mighty warrior angels that were with Margaret and me earlier; who watched over me in my dream and who gave me the wonderful glimpse of the gateway to heaven as they returned home! As they walked toward me, I noticed that each of my three angel visitors was carrying a beautifully wrapped package. A soft breeze began to rustle through the trees, prompting my wind chimes to sing their lovely lullaby, and the little tree frogs began their nightly chorus. The night sky was clear and stars twinkled overhead. "*Oh my*"—I breathed silently—"*God sure knows how to set the stage for a lovely party!*"

"Good evening, Jenn!" said Margaret, beaming, as she enveloped me in a big hug. "What a glorious night for a celebration! Our Heavenly Father sends you his dearest love and blessings, and he is so excited about tonight!" My heart thrilled as I imagined my Lord's personal involvement in this evening. "I see you remember our friends, Jenn. They did not want to miss this special time with you. Come, let's all go sit down!"

Margaret led us over to our table and chairs by the garden. As she walked with me, she leaned over and whispered mischievously in my ear, "I *love* your dress Jenn!" I gave her a playful, happy nudge in response. Four chairs covered elegantly in white silk and ribbons were placed around the table. We sat down, surrounded by the white roses and dancing, glowing orbs. The angels placed their three packages on the table. Margaret giggled as she caught me eyeing the beautifully wrapped gifts.

"Yes, my dear child, these gifts are for you, but if you can stand the suspense for just a little while longer, I have a special message for you from our Father."

I nodded, my excitement mounting.

Margaret stretched out her arms and opened her hands. "Let's all join hands together," she instructed quietly. I reached out my arms and placed each of my hands in the massive hand of one of the warrior angels, one on my left and one on my right. The warrior angels joined their hands with Margaret. As we sat in silence for a moment, the most wondrous thing happened. All three angels began to glow with a radiant white light, and then it spread over to me, so that we all sat there at the little table, enveloped in the glory light of heaven.

Then Margaret began to speak in a gentle, clear voice. "Jennifer, you have been faithful to your heart's desire to tell your story of God's presence in your life and how he speaks to you. He is delighted. This subject is very important to him, which is why he did not let you continue to set this task aside and why he sent me here to help you with it. Your testimony to the power of God's presence in your life and in the lives of all his children is powerful. You have been patient in gaining understanding of your spiritual gifts and you have learned to use them to teach others about our Lord and his plan for his Creation. He is pleased that you are showing others, through your own very personal experiences, how to recognize and listen to his voice. In the telling of your story, you have opened yourself and made yourself vulnerable, so others can see how God has worked in your life. I know that this has not been easy for you.

"What God desires more than anything else is for his children to seek him, to develop an intimate and prayerful relationship with him, to *ask* him for what they need in order to live full, joyful, complete lives. Oh, my dear child, our Father has so *much* to give to each of his beloved children! You are the delight of his heart, and his dearest wish is to be the delight of *your* heart! This has been his plan since the very Beginning."

My heart overflowed with love and humility as I sat there listening to Margaret's words. Fighting back the tears that were once again welling in my eyes, my gaze fell upon the wrapped packages on the table, and I recalled a meaningful story about the gifts God wishes to share with us. "Margaret," I said, a little shyly, "something you said just now, about how God has so much he wants to give us, reminds me of a remarkable vision someone once shared with me. Would you like to hear about it?"

"We would love to!" all three angels exclaimed at once. That made me smile! And so I told them about the *vision of the gifts.*

A woman sees herself in a room in heaven, and the room is filled with beautifully wrapped packages. As she wanders around the room to get a closer look, she realizes that they all have her name on them! The Lord is standing there watching her, and she asks him, "Lord, what are these? Are they all for me?" The Lord replies, "Yes, child, they have been up here your entire life, just waiting for you to ask for them. When you ask for a gift, it is sent to you. These are the leftover gifts that you have never asked for."

"This woman realized that she needed to free herself to ask God for his blessings and for the desires of her heart, because he so much wants to give them. In fact, he has them all ready to send!"

I continued, addressing my three angels. "I have found this to be so true in my own life. There have been countless times I have *wished* for wisdom, for peace, for discernment, for interpretation of my dreams, and so many other things. Instead, I should have taken a much more direct and personal approach with my Father and *asked*. And the key to asking is to *ask in faith, believing with all your heart that the God of Creation will provide for you.*

"After hearing this woman's story, I began writing notes to God listing my prayers and my heart's desires. I tuck them inside my Bible on the page of Matthew 21:22 where it reads, '*Whatever you ask in prayer, you will receive, if you have faith'* (ESV). I love to pull out these notes after a while and see how God has faithfully acted on my prayers. Sometimes God responds immediately, and sometimes his response may not come as quickly as I would like, but I know that God does not operate on earth time. And, there have been times when my requests seem to have gone unanswered, but then he sends me something even better than I have asked for! God always knows what I need, even when I don't."

All three angels were nodding their heads enthusiastically as I finished my story, and Margaret exclaimed "Amen! What a poignant message this vision has for all God's children. *All you have to do is ask!*"

With a sly smile, Margaret added, "And speaking of asking, I have asked someone else to join our little celebration!" She turned in her chair, looked out into the yard and called, "Come on out, sweet babies!"

Suddenly I spied three little heads peek out from behind one of the tall rosebushes. In response to Margaret's call, out pranced my three sweet dogs, happily wagging their tails! Each wore a beautiful white satin bow tied to its collar.

I clapped my hands in surprise and delight. "Hannah! Isabel! Cody! You look awesome!" My darling canine trio trotted over to our table and stood by each of the three angels.

"We could not have the party without them, Jenn! They have so graciously shared their home and backyard with us these past few days!" Margaret directed her attention to the pups as they watched her with great interest. "And to show our thanks to you, little four-legged children, we have something for you!"

A crystal bowl had appeared on the table and it was filled to the brim with heart-shaped dog treats. Each angel took a treat from the bowl and placed it on the table before them. Cody, using all the restraint he could muster, sat down before Margaret in his best 'sit' and without any prompting pronounced three carefully formed syllables: "Rhy! Rhuv! Rhoo!"

Our two mighty angel friends roared with laughter and disbelief. They asked simultaneously, "Do the other dogs talk too?"

"No"—I giggled—"but they do a very nice doggy-speak when asked."

And sure enough, as each angel commanded them to speak, Hannah and Isabel responded brilliantly with a sharp *ruff!*

The treat-giving ceremony and laughter and *ruffs* lasted for a few more minutes until I noticed the bowl was practically empty of treats.

"I hate to be a party-pooper," I playfully scolded, "but these kiddos still have to eat their dinner! I think we have had enough treats for tonight!"

Margaret snuck one final treat to Cody and then stood up. "We can't let them leave without a blessing, Jenn," she said, looking at them fondly. The other two angels stood and joined Margaret. Each angel placed a gentle hand on a dog's forehead. I was amazed at how quiet and still the dogs had become. Maybe they sensed the presence of their Creator in their new friends.

Margaret prayed, "May God bless and keep you, dear little ones, for all the days of your lives. May you always have sunshine to play in, treats to fill your tummies, and your momma's love to keep you warm and cozy at night. God loves you very much, Hannah, Isabel, and Cody!"

After a few last pats and hand licks and tail wags all around, the pups trotted off to the porch where they happily snuggled into their outside beds to wait for me.

I was so touched that Margaret had included my sweet dogs in this special evening. She really knows my heart!

Next, Margaret picked up one of the wrapped gifts from the table. She walked over to my chair and handed it to me. "Okay, Jennifer, now it is your turn for treats! This one is from me!"

The gift in my hands was wrapped in mint green paper with a pink ribbon bow. I carefully unwrapped it and set the paper aside. I opened the box and lifted out something round and flat. I turned it over, and there in my hands lay a beautiful little resin plaque. It was cream-colored and had flowers and a green vine trailing down the left side and a smaller bit of vine on the right side. The flowers were pink and blue morning glories. Carved in the middle of the plaque were the words, *Bless This Garden.*

"Oh, Margaret, thank you!" I breathed. "This is beautiful."

"You are so very welcome, dear child! And before I tell you why I gave it to you, you must open your other two gifts."

One of the mighty angels stood, selected his gift from the table and came to stand in front of me. "I present this to you, Jennifer, from the One who has been faithfully talking to you all the years of your life," he said with a beautiful smile. He placed the package gently in my hands.

The package was wrapped in dark blue-green paper with a soft, dove-gray ribbon. It felt so light that it seemed empty. Nevertheless, I carefully opened it and pulled out what looked like a thick sheet of paper. As I turned it over to look at the front, I gave a gasp of surprise. It was a painting, and it was one of mine! It was a watercolor of Jesus kneeling and praying in the Garden of Gethsemane that I did several months ago. It was my personal tribute and gift to Jesus during the season of Lent. I turned a questioning gaze to the angel in front of me. He smiled, his eyes twinkling and said, "Just wait a moment, dear one, there is one more gift."

The last angel rose from his chair and stood before me with the final gift from the table. It was wrapped in lovely pearl white paper with a light blue satin ribbon. He placed it in my hands, and I noticed that there were soft tears in his eyes as he said tenderly, "This gift, dear child, is from the One whom you honored when you began to tell Margaret your story."

I carefully took the gift from his hands and unwrapped it. My heart pounded and my hands trembled with anticipation as I pulled something hard and flat from the box. I turned it over in my hands. It was a small, plain hardcover book. I opened it and looked inside…and my heart stood still. *There, on the pages, were my very own words—my conversations with Margaret...my dreams. It was my story...my book!*

I looked up with tears in my eyes to see all three angels smiling at me and laughing softly with joy.

"Yes, Jennifer," said Margaret, her eyes twinkling like the stars, "the book you hold in your hands is *your book.* The one you have been writing with me these past few days. The last chapter is being written and added to the pages as we speak."

I shook my head in wonder and disbelief, unable to come up with anything to say that could even remotely express the joy surging through my heart. *I'm not going to have to remember everything we have talked about in order to write my book after all, because it is already written! Oh, thank you, God!*

Margaret's voice brought me back to the party. "Remember, Jenn, when you told me about hearing the voice of our Father say to you on the beach in Maine that '*it is all tied together*'?"

I nodded yes. Margaret continued.

"Tonight, dear one, heaven and earth have come together in your garden, a place of quiet beauty where God loves to spend time with you! The first gift you received tonight is a blessing for your garden. Your book was written here in the garden of your very own backyard, where we have spent much time sharing your stories and enjoying the beauty of God's creation. Your second gift is a reproduction of the painting you so lovingly created of our Lord praying in a garden. The Garden of Gethsemane is the quiet place our dearest Jesus chose to talk to his Father in heaven. Our Father would be delighted should you choose to use this painting in your book, for, just as Jesus talked with his Father in heaven, our Father in heaven is talking to you and to all of his children.

"God's love for gardens is represented in scripture from beginning to end. God created the Garden of Eden for his beloved children, Adam and Eve. He walked with them and talked with them in that beautiful place. And when the great I AM finally comes to dwell among his children once again in the new heaven and earth, a new and glorious garden will spring forth from in front of his throne, a crystal clear river of the water of life lined on either side by the trees of life, laden with luscious fruits.

"So my dear child, continue to treasure your gardens and tend to them well, for as you can see, they are much beloved of the Father. You have created your gardens with much love and thought, and what is sown in love will bloom in beauty and grace. Your gardens bring peace and respite to those who visit here. This is a lovely place where the voice of the Almighty can be heard and where his love and grace can be experienced."

I was overwhelmed by all that Margaret had tied together for me. All of this—my gardens, my painting, my book, *everything*—had been part of my Heavenly Father's plan all along! In the future, I intend to be listening even closer to his voice so as not to miss out on one second of the blessings he has in store for me!

A gentle breeze began rustling the treetops, picking up in intensity as it brushed through my backyard, ringing my wind chimes and ruffling the leaves and blossoms of the white rosebushes with the sound of a melancholy sigh. I sensed a change in the air.

Before I could even say a proper thank-you for this wonderful evening, Margaret and the two mighty angels rose from the table. As she looked at me fondly, I knew that she understood the feelings in my heart. I loved her so much and have treasured the moments we have had here at this table sharing coffee, laughter, tears, and stories of God's revealed truths. With a sinking feeling, I suspected that my beloved angel and her two friends were soon going to leave my backyard for the final time. I rose from my chair to join them.

Confirming my last thought, Margaret gently placed her hands in mine and looked into my eyes. "Jenn, it is now time for us to return home, for our assignment here is finished. You will see us again, dear one, for we are always with you—remember that I *am* your guardian angel! And who knows"—she winked mysteriously—"our Father may have other assignments for you and me in the future!" Her blue eyes danced merrily as she smiled her beautiful smile and wrapped me in a big hug.

"Thank you, all of you," I said with a full heart. "This was a wonderful party, and your gifts are precious to me. I will think of each of you every day as I sit out here in my garden. I love you all so very much!"

"We love you too, Jennifer," all three said at once. That made me smile again! Each of the mighty warrior angels gave me a big, sweet, gentle hug, and then all three angels turned and walked slowly back through the white rosebushes towards the statue of St. Francis.

As they shimmered and vanished in a soft glow of white light, my backyard was returned to its original setting—the rosebushes and glowing, dancing lights were gone.

Feeling the return of those pesky tears, I breathed a deep sigh and walked over to where the angels had just departed. Something caught my attention on the ground at the feet of St. Francis. I smiled through my tears as I recognized what it was. There on the ground lay a beautiful white rose, with no thorns. Suddenly, the air around me was filled with a sweet, clear voice that could only belong to an angel, and to my delight, she was singing a hymn that I dearly loved called *In the Garden...*

"I come to the garden alone, while the dew is still on the roses; and the voice I hear, falling on my ear; The Son of God discloses.

And he walks with me, and he talks with me, and he tells me I am his own, and the joy we share as we tarry there, None other has ever known..."

I closed my eyes and let my mind fill with the image of Jesus smiling at me and holding my hand as we listened to the hymn together here in my own garden.

All too soon, Margaret's sweet, beautiful voice faded away, and I knelt down to pick up the white rose. As I stood and brushed the tears from my face, a smile formed on my lips as I looked at the rose in my hand. I knew just what to do with it.

Epilogue

It will be good for those servants whose master finds them ready, even if he comes in the second or third watch of the night...You also must be ready, because the Son of Man will come at an hour when you do not expect him.

Luke 12:38, 40 (NIV)

Dappled sunlight sparkles through the tall pines of the dense forest, and my footsteps make barely a sound on the soft carpet of mossy earth. This looks a lot like the beloved Michigan pine forest where I vacationed in my youth. I lift my head and breathe in the pungent aroma of evergreen mixed with the musty smell of decaying leaves and pine needles. As I continue down the path I come upon a large log cabin lodge. It has two massive hinged wooden doors, which stand wide open. I step through the great doors and look around the interior of the lodge. Above me, a high-beamed ceiling soars upward and meets at the center like an A. The

floor is made of strong wooden planks. There is no furniture except for one thing that stands in the middle of the room directly in front of me. It is a huge, long, rectangular wooden table. It is so tall I can barely see over it.

I sense movement and see a doorway on the wall to the left of the table, like a big pantry door. Someone is rummaging around inside. Then he steps out. It is Jesus! He moves along the table, busily arranging items and then returns to the pantry for more. Whatever he is doing, he is totally engrossed in it. Finally, he notices my presence, and looks at me with a mixture of surprise and joy, and walks around the table to stand in front of me. "Jennifer!" He exclaims. "You are early! As you see, I am still preparing things." He puts his arm around my shoulder and gently guides me outside. He turns me toward the forest, and I see hundreds of little log houses that blend in so well with the trees that I did not notice them before. He motions to one of the houses and lovingly whispers in my ear. "Go home, child, and get yourself ready. When everything is prepared, I will call all of you to come and join me!"

Excitedly, I head off toward the little house he has selected for me, full of anticipation for the feast he has so diligently been preparing!

Will *you* hear him when he calls?

Bibliography

Thirst:

Augustine quotation: Alcorn, Randy. *Heaven.* Copyright 2004 by Eternal Perspective Ministries.

Mills, Roy. The Soul's Remembrance: Earth is not our Home. Copyright 1999 by Roy Mills.

Heart's Delight:

Piper, Reverend Don. *90 Minutes in Heaven.* Copyright 2004 by Don Piper.

Swedenborg, Emanuel (1749–56). *Arcana Coelestia 8337.* Internet reference http://www.sacred-texts.com/swd/ac/ac167.htm

Pilgrimage:

Moore, Beth. *Stepping Up: A Journey Through the Psalms of Ascent.* Copyright 2007 by LifeWay Press.

The Table Is Set:

Henry, Matthew. *Matthew Henry's Concise Commentary on the Whole Bible, Complete and Unabridged in One Volume.* Copyright 1991, 2008 by Hendrickson Publishers, Inc.

When Worlds Collide:

Alcorn, Randy. *Heaven.* Copyright 2004 by Eternal Perspective Ministries.

Hoekema, Anthony A. *The Bible and the Future.* Copyright 1979 by Grand Rapids, Eerdmans

Garden Party :

Hymn: In the Garden. C. Austin Miles. Copyright MCMXII (1912), by Hall-Mack Co.